KILLER

Center Point
Large Print

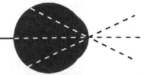

**This Large Print Book carries the
Seal of Approval of N.A.V.H.**

KILLER

Wade Everett

CENTER POINT PUBLISHING
THORNDIKE, MAINE

This Center Point Large Print edition
is published in the year 2011 by arrangement with
Golden West Literary Agency.

The text of this Large Print edition is unabridged.
In other aspects, this book may vary
from the original edition.
Printed in the United States of America
on permanent paper.
Set in 16-point Times New Roman type.

ISBN: 978-1-60285-943-2

Library of Congress Cataloging-in-Publication Data

Everett, Wade.
  Killer / Wade Everett. — Center Point large print ed.
    p. cm.
  Originally published: New York : Ballantine Books, 1962.
  ISBN 978-1-60285-943-2 (library binding : alk. paper)
  1. Large type books. I. Title.
  PS3553.O5547K55 2011
  813′.54—dc22

                                                        2010029542

Ingram 12/11 ⁴31.95

KILLER

Chapter One

In the early afternoon Burke Pine's horse took a stone bruise and Burke was forced to stop and dismount. He stood there, bent a bit by age and hard living, his jaws idly working on a cud of tobacco. Then he looked at his partner who sat loose in the saddle, hands crossed on the saddle horn.

This was a bad place to stop. Behind them were forty miles of blistering desert already smudged by shimmering risers of heat. Ahead lay another twenty miles, no better than what they had covered, and probably worse.

From his high perch in the saddle, Jim Cannon said, "Cuss a spell; I hear it helps." He said it but he knew that Burke Pine wouldn't cuss. He never cussed the things that couldn't be helped. They were hard-used men, these two, one young, one old. Their clothes were torn and dirty and they wore beards and there was half a sleeve missing in Burke Pine's shirt. Salt from much sweating rimmed the underarms of their shirts and the bands of their hats. The only thing about them that seemed unworn, untouched, were their pistols and the badges pinned to their shirts.

Burke Pine squinted his eyes and looked ahead to where the outline of mountains was barely visible through the blue veil of heat. He said,

7

"That's a far piece." Then he thoughtfully chewed his tobacco. "Can't turn the poor critter loose. Thirst is a hell of a way to die. Can't ride her, and leading her that far may cripple her for life."

"How far ahead do you think he is?" Jim Cannon asked. He was a lean man in his early twenties, a man with a quick, dangerous bent to him; there was a checked wildness in his eyes and an impatience in the way he moved as though he were pushed along by an inner force too strong to resist.

"He's ahead," Pine said. "That's all I know." He chewed some more, then stripped off the saddle and the canteens and his rifle and blanket roll. "Hate to risk a shot," he said and reached behind him for his knife. There was a moment of hesitation, then he caught the horse by the ear and opened the jugular with one motion. He let the horse go and she reared and turned, then fell. Burke Pine couldn't watch this; he turned his head and tears ran down his dirty cheeks and left runnels in the dust there.

"Time for a swig," Cannon said and stepped down, holding the reins, for the smell of blood was making his horse jumpy. He tied the reins to his wrist, then uncorked a canteen and offered it to Burke Pine.

The old man had to finger the tobacco out of his cheek before drinking, then he wiped his mouth on his sleeve. "Had that mare seven years. She was a stayer." His glance touched Jim Cannon. "It's just something else Tass Creel is going to pay for."

"If we catch him," Cannon said.

"Fourteen years now and I never been this close before," Pine said. "I'll catch him, and I'll take him back." He bent and picked up his rifle and canteen and blanket roll and turned again to the south, following the faint trail that could be a day old, or a month old.

Cannon mounted and said, "Leave the blanket roll, Burke. Ride double."

"Your horse wouldn't last five miles," the old man said.

Cannon said nothing and he knew better than to offer the horse while he walked, for the old man never asked favors, not in the three years they'd rangered together.

They moved on at a slow, steady walk, ignoring the smothering heat, knowing that this was the only way to move across so vast an expanse of wasteland. The trail they followed was faint, erased entirely by wind for long stretches, but they kept to the south and always picked it up again.

Cannon dismounted without stopping and led his horse, walking a pace behind Burke Pine. Pine was pleased that Cannon would share his misery, but he made no comment on it. The walking and the sand would eat out the seams of their boots in five miles and the sand would get in there and grind away until the blood came, and Pine was sorry that he had to walk, sorry that it made Cannon walk too, but he knew the young man, knew the strong pride there that made him share good and bad and shirk none of it.

At sundown they stopped and Cannon took some grain from his saddlebag and fed the horse. While he ate he hobbled him, then sat down in the sand. "If there was a river nearby," Cannon said, "I'd go waller in it all night long." He started to pull off his boots, then stopped. "My feet are so swollen I probably couldn't get 'em back on again." He sat spraddle-legged, bracing himself with stiffened arms. "A fire and some coffee would go good, if there was anything to burn. And if there was some coffee." He patted his pockets in a useless search for smoking tobacco.

Burke Pine said, "You might as well quit that. You was out yesterday and the day before and with six pockets, I don't guess you missed any."

"Pattin's about the same kind of habit as smokin'," Jim Cannon said. He looked off into the darkness toward the mountains. "I guess he's out there, and I guess he knows we're here."

"He knows all right," Pine said. He unrolled his blankets and spread them on the sand. In the center of his pack he had a black iron frying pan and a shallow iron stewpot with a lid. He placed the lid upside down in the sand next to the stewpot and skillet. "A man would think things like that would be too heavy to lug across the desert. And at mid-day the urge to throw the blanket roll aside is pretty strong." He chuckled softly. "The first time I seen a skillet set out, I thought that old miner was crazy. But before dawn when the temperature dropped to near freezin' and a pint of water condensed in that skillet, I made up my mind to pack 'em no matter what." He stretched out and put his hands behind his head. "When the heat bothers me and my bones feel like they're going to crack, I think of Tass Creel and remember that I'm runnin' toward, and he's runnin' from."

Jim Cannon stood up and unbuckled his shotgun chaps and spread them on the ground, then took off his pistol belt and scratched where the continued, settled weight of the gunbelt irritated the sweat and dirt. He laid the holstered pistol by his side and stretched out again. "Creel's a fool to head south through the desert," Cannon said. "I'd have fought my way through."

"There wasn't any other place for him to go," Pine said. "You've got to understand Creel to figure this. He never shot a man face to face, boy. When he broke, he knew where his chances were, and he figured it wrong, thinking I wouldn't follow him into Mexico." He sighed and reached into his pocket for some tobacco, then grunted in disgust. "Damned if I ain't out too." He massaged

11

the sore, thin muscles of his thighs. "Once Creel hits those mountains, he'll have water. Then he'll break off in any direction. Now he's got no choice but to keep south until he gets to the spring. We got to get to him before he gets his rest and leaves."

"I give the man credit for guts anyway," Jim Cannon said. "Fourteen rangers in town, and you and me walking Shatlock up the courthouse steps, a hand on each arm, and Creel puts a bullet right through his head. I give it to him for guts."

"He's good at his business," Pine said. "Any dried meat left?" He rolled over and reached for his canteen, then sat up to eat and drink.

They had their rest, five hours of it, then the bitter cold woke them and they stamped around, trying to ease the stiffness of their muscles. When they moved on, they both walked, and Pine carried the iron skillet while Cannon carried the pot and lid.

Just before dawn they stopped to carefully pour the collected water into their canteens. Jim Cannon said, "This walkin' ain't goin' to get us any closer to him."

"His horse is tuckered too," Burke Pine said.

"Maybe so, but tired or not, he's movin' faster than we are." He took a canteen off the saddle and hooked it over his shoulder. "Been thinkin' about this, Burke. This is how we're goin' to work it.

You mount up and ride on for an hour. I'll follow afoot. Then you dismount, picket the horse and go on afoot while I catch up. Then I'll mount up and catch you. We'll trade this off and on and make better time."

The old man thought about it, then said, "I'm a sergeant. I ought to have thought of that." He grinned. "Hate to admit it, Jim, but you can think a little. Me first, you say? I guess that's on account of my rank and not my age."

"What else?" Cannon said and took his Winchester. As soon as Pine swung up, he slapped the horse and then began walking.

When the sun came up it turned off hot right away and Cannon followed the fresh tracks and finally saw the horse ahead. Burke Pine was out there in that shimmering waste, walking on, and they worked it that way through the intense heat of the day. In the early grayness of evening they joined together in the first rocky reaches of the foothills.

Pine said, "About three miles to water." He pointed to higher ground well ahead. "There's a spring there. And a pool. Never dries up. Creel's there."

"Are we goin' in tonight?"

"In the mornin' he'll be gone," Pine said. "If he ain't already." He drank from the canteen, but did not empty it, and when Cannon drank a little too long, Pine pulled it away. "Don't empty that before you're dippin' your hands in that spring, boy. Creel's sittin' up there, waitin' for us. He knows we've got to reach it, and he means to see that we don't."

"I didn't think," Cannon said. "Sorry, Burke."

"Don't be," Pine said and led the way up the draw. As he walked he let his soft voice drift back. "It'll pay us to be a bit cautious approachin' the spring. Since you've got a wife, I'll make the first move. And now I don't want to hear any argument. Somebody's got to make it, and these old bones couldn't take another long run if Creel breaks away. You understand?"

"Sure, Burke."

They spent nearly an hour slowly working up the draw, climbing to higher, more barren and rocky ground. Then Burke Pine stopped and they wedged a picket pin in a crack in the rocks and left the horse there and went on.

Burke stopped again and this time he spoke in little more than a whisper. "Ahead there, maybe two hundred yards, is the spring." He stopped and listened. In some nearby brush a small animal moved and insects whirred in the darkness but there was no other sound. Pine patted Cannon on the arm and went on, moving in a crouch and taking his time. Behind him, Cannon wondered why they didn't come in some other way, then supposed that this draw was the only way into the spring. It was something to think about, for if that was the case, Tass Creel would have to fight his way out.

Pine made his mistake, a small sound as he slipped and caught himself, and it was enough, for farther ahead, and much higher up there was a blossom of muzzle flame and the boom of a .45-70 trap-door Springfield. The bullet struck between the two men and whined away; they sprawled for cover, each moving in the opposite direction.

Cannon went into the rocks and started climbing, hoping to work his way around to Creel's position. He spent ten minutes in slow, skin-tearing work, then Creel fired again at some sound Burke Pine made below near the spring.

The night was dark, almost a thick blackness, but Cannon found that he could make out the shadow of objects and he had Creel's position pretty well set in his mind. As near as he could tell, the man hadn't moved between shots, which led Cannon to believe that he was in a sheltered pocket of some kind.

He had to work slowly, carefully, feeling every step of the way, searching the ground for stones that might roll and give him away, feeling for loose rock ahead so he could move another foot ahead.

For what seemed an hour he inched along and Creel did not fire again although from time to time Pine tossed rocks to make some noise.

Finally Cannon could make out his target, Creel crouched low among the rocks; he was at a slightly lower level than Cannon and he almost fell on top of the man before he saw him. Six feet separated them and Cannon lay there, making no sound, studying the situation. He could see Creel's rifle, a long-barreled officer's model with a detachable telescopic sight, and he wondered whether he should just shoot him or jump him. Jumping would be risky in the dark and uncertain terrain, and shooting would be something Pine wouldn't like, for he wanted Creel to stand trial.

Cannon felt around until he found a rock the size of a cocoanut, then he lifted it, gauged his distance carefully and let it arc up. He heard the thud as it landed, striking Creel a glancing blow on the side of the head, and it was enough to stun the man, enough to allow Cannon to jump down, disarm him, and search him for a pistol. When he found none, he yelled, "Burke, I got him!"

From a spot not ten feet away, Burke Pine said, "No use yellin'. I ain't deaf."

The nearness of the voice made Cannon jump, then Pine laughed and came into the pocket and helped lift Creel, who could not quite stand by himself. They took him below to the spring and tied him up; then Cannon gathered brush and built a fire.

Pine went through Creel's pockets for tobacco and found a sack of dust. He pinched some and put it in his cheek, then handed the sack and makings to Jim Cannon.

"Fill the canteens before you muddy up the spring takin' a bath," Pine said. He spoke to Cannon but he was looking at Tass Creel.

Cannon finished his cigaret making and lit it and drew deeply. Then he looked at Creel. "He ain't very big, is he?"

"Big enough to shoot your head off at five hundred yards," Pine said. The firelight spread in a widening circle, plainly illuminating the spring. Tass Creel sat on the ground, his hands tied behind him, and he looked at these two men. His eyes were gray and his hair was gray and he had a round, seemingly boneless face and a bland, harmless expression. In height he was little more than five foot six, yet he was stocky like a well-fed farmer. He wore torn jeans and a gray work shirt and his pants were held up with suspenders.

"I thought you was Mexican bandits," Creel said. His voice was soft, a little high-pitched, but not from nervousness. "I wouldn't have shot at you had I know you were the law. Why don't you untie me? I don't mean any harm."

"Is that a fact?" Burke Pine said. He laughed and jerked his thumb toward the spring. "Go soak, boy. I'll stay with Creel until you come back. Go on, that's an order."

"I won't be long," Cannon said.

"Take your time. We've got plenty now."

Burke Pine squatted by the fire and watched Creel and he could hear Cannon splashing in the water. It was almost a pain in the old man for he knew how good it felt, biting cold, a balm for his torn feet and dried-out body. Yet he could wait, for he had Tass Creel to look at.

"Texas Rangers got no business in Mexico," Creel said gently. It was his manner to be gentle, to be soft-spoken, and he smiled winningly and when he did it was difficult for a man to think bad of him, or not like him.

"What business have you got here?" Pine asked.

"Thought I'd get some hunting," Creel said.

"Where's your gear?"

"Lost it."

Burke Pine laughed. "Try again." Cannon left the spring and handed the old man a canteen; he drank deeply and poured the rest of it over his head, letting it soak his shirt and waist.

Cannon said, "He don't look like much, does he?"

"You said that before," Pine commented. He studied the round, innocent face of Tass Creel, and the bland, trusting eyes. Creel was not a man who showed his fifty-odd years; there was an ageless quality about him, and only the gray hair indicated that he was getting on. "Sit down, boy," Pine said.

"Ain't you goin' to take your soak?"

"In time. No rush," Pine said. He patted the ground and Cannon squatted. "You look good at him, boy. Twenty-eight years ago he was a sniper in the Union army, a young fella with fuzz on his cheeks and no trade except potting another man at four hundred yards. How many men have you killed, Creel?"

"Why," Creel said, his face going slack with surprise, "I've never killed anyone in my life. That's the God's truth." He looked from one to the other. "Say, are you fellas arresting me or somethin'?"

"Are you just understanding that?" Cannon asked.

"But what for? Don't a man have a right to know?"

"The murder of Price Shatlock while he was in the custody of the Texas Rangers," Burke Pine said. "Now I suppose you're going to tell me that ain't so."

"That's just what I'm tellin' you," Creel said. "I never saw Shatlock in my life." He blew out a long breath. "When was I supposed to have done this terrible thing?"

"Three weeks ago," Pine said. "At Rock Springs. You stood by the window of the second floor of the feed store a block away from the courthouse, and while we led Shatlock up the steps to testify, you blew his head nearly off with that .45-70."

"I suppose," Creel said, "you've got a witness that seen me do it."

"Nope," Pine said. "But we finally found a kid who saw a lone man carrying a long rifle leave town and take the south road. We've been on your trail since then."

"You've made a terrible mistake," Creel said. "I've never been arrested in my whole life."

"You are now," Jim Cannon said drily.

"It's a mistake," Creel said simply. "Just a terrible mistake. You'll find that out." He shook his head as though dumbfounded, yet he seemed to possess an infinite patience that justice would prevail and prove him innocent. "All right, I'll go back with you."

"You got no choice," Pine said.

"You don't understand. I'll go back willingly to clear my name." He looked at Pine. "You call me Creel. That's not my name."

"What is it then?" Cannon asked.

"Moss McKitrick. I'm not from Texas. Just passed through. Hell, you can check that. Just wire my wife in Ashland, Kansas. Ask anybody there. I've lived there for eighteen years. Got a farm outside of town. Ask anybody." He spoke without raising his voice, and his manner, his expression, was sincere, difficult to doubt. He watched Burke Pine and saw the complete inflexibility of the old man, so he turned to Jim Cannon. "Young fella, I'm appealing to you now.

Do I look like this Tass Creel or something? Is that why I'm arrested?"

"I never saw Creel," Cannon said. "Burke, you never laid eyes on him either." He hesitated. "We could have made a mistake, like he says."

"We could have," Burke Pine admitted, "but we didn't. We'll go back to Rock Springs and prove it."

"You'll prove me innocent," the prisoner said. He fell silent and Burke Pine got up and went to the spring for his bath and Cannon noticed that he unholstered his long-barreled .44 and laid it on a rock where it would be handy while he washed.

Cannon rolled another cigaret, then started to put the sack in his pocket and stopped. He reached out and stuffed it into Creel's pocket.

"I'd thank you to roll me one," Creel said, smiling. Cannon took the tobacco, made the smoke, and replaced the sack in Creel's pocket. Then he lit it and put it between the man's lips. "I sort of thought you had less of a heavy hand than your partner," Creel said. "But you sure hurt my head with that rock."

"You was shootin'."

"I know," Creel said. "A bad thing for a man to be so suspicious in a strange country. If I hadn't done that—" He shrugged. "Your partner hates this fella, Creel. Would you tell me why?"

"Because he ain't ever been caught, I guess," Cannon said.

21

"Is he goin' to go on callin' me Creel?"

"Guess so, until he's proved different," Cannon said. "I'm just a corporal. He's a sergeant and I take his orders, mister."

"I understand and there's no hard feelin's. This Creel is a killer?"

"A paid killer," Cannon said. "Some say he's murdered fifteen men. Some say more, but fifteen seems a good number for one man to have put away without a shot havin' been fired back." He reached out, took the cigarette from Creel's mouth, flicked off the ash and put it back. "He's what you'd call a hired assassin. Did a lot of killing for the cattlemen factions fifteen or so years ago, around 1880. Before my time. Burke knows about it. He was a Wyoming sheriff then. Nobody ever went to jail for it."

"Is that what he lives for? To put men in jail?"

"Well, you put the bad ones in and leave the good ones out," Cannon said. "There's nothing wrong with that." He took a final pull on his cigaret and then crushed it out. "You don't look like the kind of a man who'd kill for money. Still, you got a mighty fancy rifle there, friend."

"It's an excellent hunting gun," Creel said. "But you don't believe that."

"Can't say what I really believe," Cannon said. "I just catch 'em and the juries decide the rest."

"Have you ever wondered if you'd arrested innocent men and had them sentenced to prison?"

"Nope," Cannon said. "What good would it do if I did?"

Burke Pine came back clad in his torn underwear; his clothes were wet from washing and he spread them by the fire to dry out. "I'll take the first watch," he said, buckling on his pistol belt.

Tass Creel watched him, then said, "How many men have you shot in the line of duty?"

"A few," Pine said drily. "Especially when they try to get away."

"I wouldn't do that," Creel said.

"That I know for sure," Pine said, and sat down to guard the prisoner.

Chapter Two

Burke Pine remained at the spring for two days, more to rest the horses than anything else; they found Creel's horse picketed farther up the draw and brought him into camp. They made Creel walk between them and Pine pushed east some thirty miles to the Mexican army post near the village of Allende. There he bought another horse, some supplies and clothes and stayed a day because it was a sociable thing to do with Mexicans.

The major in command didn't ask too many questions about Burke Pine's authority to be in Mexico and there was no demand to see papers; the Mexican army and the Rangers had a working agreement that cut through governmental red tape and put more than a few bad men, Mexican and American, behind bars.

Mounted and leading a pack horse with sufficient water and supplies, the journey back across the desert was at least tolerable, although not comfortable. Six days later they rode into the ranger camp near Rock Springs and placed Tass Creel in the guardhouse.

And when Burke Pine wrote his report, he reluctantly admitted that Creel had been a model prisoner, giving them no trouble and making no attempt to escape.

Sleep, a good meal, a bath and the work of a razor transformed Pine and Cannon into acceptable human beings and they met on the steps of the headquarters before going in to make a verbal report. Pine brushed at his waterfall mustache and looked around the camp. The only permanent buildings were the guardhouse and headquarters; the rest was tents and pole corral and messhall under the trees by the creek, and the flagpole with the colors of the State of Texas hanging limp in the motionless air. Burke Pine said, "You've turned off quiet, Jim. This last week you've hardly said two dozen words." He glanced at his friend. "Creel?"

Cannon rolled a cigaret before speaking. "To tell you the truth, Burke, the man bothers me. You and me, we've chased and caught our share and some we shot it out with. Others we fetched back. Last year, when we went to New York State to bring back that fella who'd done in his wife with a hatchet, we had to watch him like hawks sharin' a chicken. Even then he tried four breaks before we reached Kansas." He shook his head in puzzlement. "Creel gave us no trouble at all. Fact is, he was a help, cookin' the meals, even handcuffed. And the things he said, Burke, about his friends and family, well, it's put some doubt in my mind about him really bein' Creel."

"I seen him workin' on you," Pine said softly. "Well, let's go in and see what the captain's got to say. I'd hate to think I've got to start all over, but if I got to, then I will."

Jim Cannon flipped his cigaret into the yard. "You've just got to see this man hung, don't you, Burke?"

"Yeah, I got to," Pine said and went on in.

Captain Nathan Eiler commanded Company B, Texas Frontier Battalion, and he was a young man who had put aside a comfortable career in law to become a peacemaker; that was the distinction he liked to draw, peacemaker rather than lawman. He recalled vividly the wildness of the 'Eighties, when a lawman operated only on a broad base, concerning himself with major crimes and letting go the little things that assured no one of any real peace. But this was 1894 and peace officers were into a new era where the civil courts took precedence over the criminal courts; more men were charged with small offenses, and a new word, misdemeanor, was coming into the lawman's vocabulary.

Eiler was a rather slight man, graying early at the temples, and he wore a dense, dark mustache, clipped short. His taste in clothes ran to dark suits and peppermint shirts.

As soon as Pine and Cannon came into the office, Eiler waved them into chairs. He said, "See you're both still limping. You've been seeing the surgeon about those feet?"

"Yes, sir," Pine said. He took some cut plug

from his pocket, whittled off a piece and put it in his mouth.

Nathan Eiler frowned and Cannon said, "He can't talk without tobacco in his mouth, captain. The chewin' gets his jaws to movin' and he talks without much extra effort."

"That's the damnedest excuse for a bad habit I ever heard," Eiler said. He opened a manila folder and glanced at it. "Burke, I've been going over your file on Creel. Let's talk about it. We've got a man, but is he Creel?"

"I say he is," Pine said flatly. "You want to read the record or do you want me to recite it?"

Nathan Eiler frowned. "Burke, I've never asked you why catching this man has been so important to you. But I'm asking now."

"If you mean, why I'll never give up, I'll tell you. It's there in the record, but it's between the lines, sort of. Creel had a reputation before he came to Wyoming, captain. He must have had because the job he did there was big, and professional, because he made no mistakes at all. Or none anyway that he figured on." He pointed to the folder on Eiler's desk. "The killing in Wyoming is the first I lay directly on Creel's doorstep. The ones before, in Colorado and Kansas and Missouri I lay to Creel because they all follow the same pattern; a man is shot dead and no one ever finds out who did it." He got up and opened the window to spit, then came back and sat down. "It's there in the record; I was sheriff then, in 1879. Texas cattle and Texas money were pouring in and the little man was being pushed out. The biggest man around those parts was Cliff Orland. He wasn't big in land or money, but he was big in the influence and good sense he had. Orland and I were friends, good friends, and he wouldn't give an inch to the Texas pressure. They tried burning him and got hurt. They tried to pick a fight with him in town and we stood back to back and left dead men in the street. I heard they were bringing in a man to do the job, but Cliff wasn't afraid of anything he could see or hear. The trouble was, he never saw Creel, or heard him. He was leavin' for town and he came out of his house with his wife and turned to kiss her goodbye and Creel put a bullet right through his head. It killed her too."

When Pine hesitated, Nathan Eiler said, "Are you going to stop there, Burke?"

The old man glanced at Cannon, then said, "Annie Orland was the only woman in the world I ever wanted, and she belonged to my best friend. I saw the summer sky in her eyes and heard the wind sigh when she spoke; she was more than a woman to me, Nathan. She was the gentleness a man like me never gets in his life, the only spot of comfort I ever saw in a comfortless world. And Tass Creel killed her with a bullet in the brain." He sighed and looked at his gnarled hands. "A rider found them on the porch the next day. I turned that country upside down, captain, and all I found out was that a drifter had seen a man riding along with a long-barreled rifle. That was three days after the killing. The Texas men didn't know anything, least of all Price Shatlock. I knew he was the one who paid for the job, but I couldn't prove it. That winter I found one of the Texas riders and while he was drunk, he told me about a man Shatlock had hired. That's how I learned his name: Tass Creel."

Nathan Eiler sat for a moment in silence, then he said, "I don't think anyone ever knew this, Burke."

"No one ever did. Not Orland, or his wife."

Eiler nodded and tapped the record. "But Tass Creel is like a myth, Burke. No home, no past, nothing to tie to. Where does he come from? Where does he go afterward?"

"Five years later," Pine said, "Creel killed again. This time it was one of the big Texas men, one of Shatlock's friends. I was a ranger then and you've got all the information in the record. Shatlock had had a falling out, and Creel did the job for him, but who could prove it? The next year, Shatlock took over some more property."

"There's no doubt Shatlock was behind the hiring," Eiler said. "He's been involved in all of these killings, from Orland's to the last." He read a bit. "Two more of Shatlock's friends were killed in the same way, a bullet through the head. Here it is; Kyle Dixon was the last. Killed while driving to town with his son. No one knows what happened to the boy because he was never found." He closed the folder. "Burke, it's a dirty record, but damned little in it about Tass Creel. What's there would fit ten thousand men, and all given by people who had seen, at a distance mind you, a man riding with a long rifle." He laid his hands flat on the desk. "I think we'd better question the prisoner. Cannon, will you tell the sergeant of the guard to escort him here?"

"Yes, sir," Cannon said and left the office.

Nathan Eiler pulled at his lip. "What have we got to hold him on, Burke? Suspicion?" He looked for a moment out the window then said, "He claims he ain't Creel. We can hold him while we check his story." He ran his fingers through his dense hair. "Burke, unless we come up with something to support his identity as Tass Creel, we're going to have to turn him loose."

"If I had some time," Burke Pine said, "I might just do that. Price Shatlock is dead because he was going to talk. To me that means that some of the old land grabbers are getting tired of holding onto secrets they've kept hidden for twenty years. Shatlock was going to spill the beans. Could be some others are inclined to talk. I'm thinking that Creel's been seen, talked to by one or more of these men. If they pointed a finger at the man we're holding and said, 'He's the one,' then we'd have our case."

"You find me that man then," Eiler said. "There's Whitlow, Keene, and Maybry still alive. If someone hired Creel to kill Shatlock and paid him for it, it had to be one of them. It could also be that they've seen Creel and can identify him." He stopped talking as Cannon and the sergeant of the guard came in with the prisoner.

"Take off his handcuffs," Eilers said. "You can wait outside, sergeant. Fetch Mr. Creel a chair, Cannon." He folded his hands and looked at the prisoner whose cheeks had been bladed to a clean pinkness. He had the skin of a younger man, smooth, not susceptible to tanning.

"Captain, I'd like to make a request," Creel said.

"All right, what is it?"

"My name is Moss McKitrick. You're going to find that out soon enough. I'd like to be called by my right name." He smiled pleasantly. "After all, captain, it will be just something less to apologize for when you turn me loose."

"You seem sure of being turned loose," Pine said.

McKitrick looked at him. "Why, I'm positive, sergeant. You've got the wrong man."

"Perhaps you'd like to answer some questions," Eiler said.

"Anything you want to ask," McKitrick said. He spread his plump hands, a gesture of undeniable appeal. "I haven't a thing to hide, captain. My life's an open book with every page for you to read."

"According to a witness, you were seen in Rock Springs on the day Price Shatlock was killed," Eiler said.

McKitrick shook his head. "That's not possible because I didn't go into Rock Springs. And I wouldn't know what day that was because I'd lost track of them. I did pass near the town though. A mile or so, I'd judge."

"I can send for the boy who saw you," Eiler said flatly. "Should I do that?"

"No, it won't be necessary," McKitrick said sincerely. "I recall seeing a boy, somewhere around fifteen or sixteen. He was coming from the direction of the creek and he had a .22 rifle with him, carrying it on his shoulder like a soldier." He frowned and thought a minute. "He was some piece off the trail, but I recall that he had kind of sandy hair. He saw me and I saw him and I rode on and never looked twice at him."

Eiler looked at Burke Pine, then said, "That's the way it was, Mr. McKitrick." He sighed and lit a cigar, then offered one to the prisoner, who shook his head. "You have a very unusual rifle, Mr. McKitrick. An officer's model Springfield fitted with an excellent sight. Isn't that unusual for a man to carry when nearly everyone uses a repeater?"

"A man likes what he likes," McKitrick said. "I'm a good shot and I hunt every year."

"In Mexico?"

"Yes, many times," McKitrick said.

"The horse you were riding wore a haired-over range brand," Eiler said. "Where did you get the animal? I ask because the brand has a Texas registry."

"I bought him in Sonora, from a man I never saw before," McKitrick said. "I rode the train there, got off, had a meal, and bought the horse. Captain, have you telegraphed my wife yet? I have a family and they'll worry if they don't hear from me."

"We'll make the proper inquiry," Eiler assured him. "Mr. McKitrick, according to your statement to Sergeant Pine, you are a farmer."

"Yes, sir, I am."

"You don't look like a farmer."

McKitrick smiled. "How does a farmer look, sir?" He spread his soft hands. "The Lord has blessed me with plenty, captain. For some years now I have rented out my land to tenants, who work for me and share in the good things that come from the earth." He closed his eyes and seem to pray briefly. Then he opened them and said, "You will find, when the truth is known, that I'm a God-fearing man who has toiled hard for what I have. And I would appreciate it, sir, if you let me have a Bible in my cell. I'm used to reading from the Scripture every day."

Burke Pine made a growling noise in his throat

and said, "He's been talkin' like that ever since we took him prisoner."

Nathan Eiler shot him an irritated glance. "I've never knocked a man because he had religion," he said. "You'll have a Bible."

"How come you didn't have one when we found you?" Cannon asked.

"I had one on my pack horse but it was lost," McKitrick said.

"Captain, can I ask a question or two?" Pine asked. Eiler nodded and Burke Pine hunched around in his chair. "Some years ago Tass Creel killed two men in Texas, Kyle Dixon and Race Tanner. I happened to be in the locality and I made an effort to capture Creel, but he got away by going south. Later, I discovered that he crossed the Rio and then the desert into Mexico. Now it struck me then that only a fool or a man who knew where water was on the other side would cross that sand, so I made it my business to scout out that water. That's how come I knew where you were going and what the spring was like."

"Many men must know that spring," McKitrick said.

"Tass Creel knew it," Pine said.

"I can't say what this man, Tass Creel, knows," McKitrick said. He looked at Nathan Eiler. "Captain, surely you have some way of identifying this killer. A photograph or—"

"None's ever been took," Pine interrupted. Then he bunched his eyebrows. "Captain, how much longer do you expect to be here?"

"I suppose a half hour or a little more. Why?"

"Well, I'd like to be excused," Pine said.

Eiler nodded and Pine went out. Then the captain said, "Mr. McKitrick, I suppose you have some means of identifying yourself."

"No, I haven't. On a hunting trip a man doesn't have to prove who he is, usually."

"That's true," Eiler said and drew paper and pencil to him. "Would you give me the name of the peace officer near your home?"

"Owen Henry, sheriff," McKitrick said. "I've known him for fifteen years."

Eiler wrote it down. "And the names of two other reliable people?"

"George Mundy, postmaster. Fred Ball, general store. Both men have known me at least fifteen years, maybe longer." He smiled pleasantly.

"Ashland, Kansas?" Eiler asked.

"That's right. My wife's name is Clara. I have two sons, Wyley, and Burgess. He's named after my wife's father. A man respected by all."

"Is he living?"

"No, he died five years ago. Stroke."

"I think," Eiler said, "in the absence of any identification on you that it might be advisable if someone came here as a reliable witness and identified you."

35

"That's putting someone to a lot of trouble and needless expense, ain't it?" McKitrick asked.

"Under the circumstances, I hardly see how it can be avoided. Tass Creel is a sought-after man, one any peace officer would like to catch, although his life has been so secret that I doubt there is even a wanted poster on him anywhere. Now you were taken under at least unusual circumstances. I am willing to accept your version, pending proof, but it is also possible that you are Tass Creel and that you assumed the name of McKitrick."

"Would I dare do that?"

"Creel is a bold man. He'd do anything."

"Would I invite exposure if I were lying?"

Nathan Eiler frowned. "Not likely, but it is a question hard to answer. I think in a week or ten days we'll know. If your story checks out, you'll be free to go."

"Minus some time in your cell, and a bump on my head where this man hit me with a rock," McKitrick said.

"We always have to make some mistakes to be right at all," Eiler said. "This is a very serious matter; I'm sure you realize that. Price Shatlock was a big man in Texas and some dust is being raised to find his killer. Also, he was in the custody of the Texas Rangers who were taking what we thought to be adequate precautions against such a shooting. Shatlock warned us that an attempt would be made, and he feared Tass Creel."

"He must have told you a great deal about this man," McKitrick said.

"No, he didn't, other than the fact that he had had business with Creel in the past."

McKitrick shook his head. "You would think a man like that would be easy to find, captain. Surely a description of him—"

"We have that, ten years old," Eiler said. "He's stocky, about your height, but so are thousands of men. Yes, there are men alive who could identify him, but they'll never come forward, for to do so they'd have to admit they paid him to murder. And no man is going to hang just for the pleasure of seeing another get his neck stretched."

"I can understand that," McKitrick said.

Eiler had other questions he wanted answered, questions about McKitrick's family, about his farm and the town where he lived, all things that would be checked and if there was any flaw in the answers, Eiler would want to know why.

Finally he was through and sent Cannon over to the surgeon, who kept a spare Bible. The surgeon was surprised for he thought Cannon was getting the Word, and Cannon took the Bible and left; he didn't like the surgeon's humor.

As he was recrossing the parade ground, he saw Pine riding in and he had someone with him. They stopped by the porch and the man got down from his buggy and hurriedly began to erect a tripod and camera.

Cannon came up to Pine and asked, "What's going on?"

"Tass Creel's going to get his picture taken."

"He says he's Moss McKitrick and can prove it."

"As far as I'm concerned, he could be the very Devil himself, and still be Tass Creel." He looked at the photographer who was filling his flash tray. "About ready?"

"Yes, sir. Where's the subject?"

"He'll come out that door," Pine said and started up the steps. Then he backed down as the door opened and the sergeant of the guard herded McKitrick ahead of him. The flash went off with a *woooof* and a cloud of smoke and McKitrick blinked, then a look of rage came into his face and he lunged off the porch, trying to kick over the camera and tripod.

The sergeant hauled him up short, and then McKitrick was completely composed, his expression again pleasant and serene. Eiler, who heard the commotion, came out and spoke to Burke Pine.

"What the hell's going on here?"

"Mr. McKitrick just got his picture took," Pine said. He patted the photographer on the shoulder. "That'll do, Elmer. I'll take a dozen, and get 'em to me right away."

"How much indignity does a man have to suffer?" McKitrick said.

"You got pretty violent for a minute there," Pine said. "Especially over just getting your picture took."

"I thought it was for the newspapers," McKitrick said. "I didn't want my picture in the paper, that's all."

"My, now," Pine said, "you got an answer for everything, ain't you?"

"That's enough of that, sergeant," Eiler said. "All right, take him back to his cell. And you stick around, Burke; I want a word with you."

McKitrick was taken away and when he was out of earshot, Eiler said, "That was pretty smart of you, Burke. Send me the bill for the photographs."

"I intended to," Pine said.

Eiler smiled. "Figure on showing a few of those around to some of the big men in Texas?"

"Big and little," Pine admitted. "And I'll get somebody to talk."

"They'll be scared to."

"I guess, but I've learned this about men. A man can get too scared to talk, then you scare him a little more and he reverses himself and talks his fool head off. Shatlock was going to. Too bad he didn't live long enough to tell us what scared him so bad."

Chapter Three

Captain Eiler gave Jim Cannon several telegrams to take to town and send, and Burke Pine got on the train for El Paso, and then Jim Cannon went to his house on the edge of town, a small, two storey frame house set among the trees and surrounded by a wrought iron fence. He paused by the front gate, his hand on the latch, then he swung it open and listened to it squeak. He stood there and waited and looked at the house and considered himself a lucky man.

The front door opened and his wife ran out. He went up the path, met her half way, picked her up and whirled her about, then walked in the house with her, his arm around her. He hung up his hat and gunbelt and sat down in a parlor chair with a sigh of relief. A six-month old baby slept in a crib in the center of the room, and Cannon bent forward to study him, a slow smile building on his face.

"He ain't growed much in five weeks. Don't you feed him enough, Jane?"

"He eats like a horse wrangler," she said, sitting on the arm of his chair. She was a plump woman in her early twenties, with light brown hair and a full, sensitive mouth. He put his arm around her and she took tobacco out of his pocket and rolled a cigaret for him. "Did you get the man you were after?" she asked.

"We got a man," Jim Cannon said, "but I wonder if he's the one we went after." He lit his cigaret and drew on it a moment. "I decided to be a deputy sheriff because I was tired of bunkhouses and cow camps, and I went into the rangers for security, a steady job with fair pay and a chance for advancement. The first man I ever arrested ran because he was guilty, and most all of 'em have looked guilty or acted guilty or been caught in the act. This fella is different, Jane. Hanged if I can put my finger on it, but he makes me feel that I'm doin' him a real injustice, one I won't be able to wipe out by sayin' I'm sorry I put him to so much trouble."

She bent a bit to look at his face. "Isn't it possible for a man to look innocent and be guilty, Jim?"

"Sure, and he can look guilty and be innocent." He snubbed out his smoke in a glass dish. Then he laughed and got up and put his arms around her and kissed her. "But I didn't come home to bother you with this."

"What bothers you bothers me," she said.

"This is my home," he said. "It ain't Company B headquarters. My problems don't belong here."

"How are you and Burke Pine getting along?"

He looked at her, surprised. "Why, good. He and I seem to hit it off fine. He likes his way but I don't begrudge a man that." His eyebrows bunched into a frown. "How come you ask?"

41

"While you were gone, I went over to Captain Eiler's house and had dinner with him and his wife. She told me that Burke's never been able to keep a partner for long. She remarked about it because you've been with him longer than anyone, and she considers you a most unusual and remarkable man because of it."

"Burke and I've never had a bit of trouble," Cannon said. "He's not much for cozyin' up to a person, I know that, and the first four months we didn't say much to each other, but then we got in that tangle with the train robbers near Lamesa and afterward his attitude changed. His ways didn't change, but his attitude toward me did. After that I was a partner, not someone who followed him around to back him up. It was Burke Pine who saw that I got corporal's pay. We get along."

"Do you like him, Jim?"

He looked at her carefully. "Sure I do. Why?"

"Burke's not like you, Jim. When you come home, you leave your job behind. It's all he has and if he ever finds what he's looking for, all the steam will go out of him. A man's life has to have more to it than just a search for something."

"Tass Creel?"

"If that's what it is."

"I think so," Jim Cannon said. Then he frowned as he smiled. "Dang it, now you're getting me to worrying about it."

• • •

Cannon spent three days working around his house; he painted the shutters and back porch and dug weeds in his garden and he didn't think much about Tass Creel or Burke Pine until a ranger came to the house and told him that Eiler wanted him to report back to duty. To Cannon this meant the cessation of one life and the commencement of another, and it might be that he would be gone five hours or five months; he never had any way of knowing. But it would be putting his family aside and perhaps living out of his blankets, and it could mean danger or dull boredom; it was always something unexpected.

His wife accepted this for it was his job, and she knew the frontier, knew the kind of work men did and she knew it was a good job, better than working cattle or dry farming or working for the railroad.

Cannon said his goodbyes, bounced the baby once more, then saddled his horse and rode out to company headquarters. Captain Eiler was in his office and Cannon went right in and sat down.

Eiler had two telegrams on his desk and a drawn expression on his face. He said, "Jim, I've come to a fork in the road and I hardly know which way to go."

"Sounds like a fifty-fifty chance," Cannon said, grinning. "And captain, there have been times when I'd have grabbed onto odds as good as that."

"You're a good peace officer," Eiler said. "That's why I wanted to talk to you before I made my next move." He picked up a telegram. "This is from Sheriff Owen Henry. I sent him a complete description of Moss McKitrick and Henry assures me that this is Moss McKitrick, who left his place a month ago to go hunting."

"How about the picture Pine had taken?"

"I've already mailed him one and asked him to identify it," Eiler said. He picked up another telegram. "I sent this to a man I know in Kansas, a man I can rely on. It says that there is a Sheriff Owen Henry."

Cannon seemed surprised. "Did you think there wasn't?"

"Oh, I was pretty sure I'd get a reply from Owen Henry," Eiler said. "Only I wanted to make sure he was really the sheriff. Creel wouldn't be the first man who'd ever rigged up false identification." He pushed the telegrams aside and tapped a pencil on his desk. "Damn it, Cannon, this whole thing smells."

"It looks like McKitrick is what he says," Cannon said.

"Doesn't it though? It looks like we've made an honest mistake and detained an innocent man. But then again, the pieces are falling together too nicely. Do you know what I mean?"

"Yes, sir, I think I do. McKitrick said he went to Mexico to hunt, but that didn't look like game country to me. Maybe some wild pigs, but that's all, and you shoot those at spittin' range when they charge out of the brush. The shorter barrel you got on your rifle, the better it is. I've hunted 'em with a shotgun using slugs."

"Exactly my thinking," Eiler said. "So I sent a telegram to Colonel Ortega at the military post at Allende. His reply was that wild boar was about the only game in those mountains." He scrubbed his hand across his cheek. "Now that doesn't make sense, does it?"

"No, sir," Cannon said. "I chased that fella, captain, and he was no farmer on a jaunt. He had desert savvy. Plenty trail sense. So with what you said, I figure he's too smart not to know what kind of game he'd find in the Serranias del Burros."

Nathan Eiler smiled. "Jim, you've got the right idea. All right, let's do something about it."

"You name it, captain."

"I've sent a photograph to Owen Henry for identification. It went out on last night's train, so he should have it day after tomorrow. Maybe the day after that. Anyway, it'll be four days before I get a reply, and I can sit on that for a week. You see, I'm trying to buy some time for Burke Pine. I want you to cash in on it too."

"That's not very much, captain."

"I know, and I'll do the best I can to extend it. Frankly, I've asked for a preliminary hearing. After all, Shatlock was a big shot and this will soothe his friends at the state capital. Judge Rainsford will be here in ten days to two weeks. That's all the time I can give you."

"Well, we'll do the best we can with what we have," Cannon said. "Just what do you want me to do?"

"I want you to find a break in Moss McKitrick's story."

"In Kansas?"

"In hell itself if you have to go there," Eiler said. "Look at it this way, Jim: if ever a man had a reason to get Tass Creel, it's Burke Pine. Also we've got Burke's record; he's made damned few mistakes in his career as a peace officer. Somehow, in spite of the evidence, I think he's right now. But we've got to prove it, Jim." He reached for some papers. "Give these to my clerk; they're your travel orders. He'll give you some money. Take the freight out this afternoon; we can't waste time waiting for the northbound passenger train tomorrow. And wire me when you change towns, Jim. I may need you back here in a hurry if the hearing starts."

"Yes, sir." He got up and put on his hat. "Anything else?"

"Bring me some evidence," Eiler said.

Cannon nodded. "Some of the questions I'll ask are liable to stir up some old dust, captain. You start diggin' back through the years and there's no tellin' what you'll find out."

"I've never been afraid of ghosts," Eiler said, and turned to the paper work he was trying to catch up on. Then he leaped from his chair, snatched up a folder from his desk and caught Cannon just as he was going off the porch. "Here's a print of the photograph Burke took. Take it along." He handed it to Cannon and went back into his office.

Judge Michael Rainsford arrived in the late afternoon and a ranger took one of the ambulances to the station to get him. That evening he had dinner with Eiler and his family and afterward they went to the parlor to talk; Rainsford wanted to read Eiler's brief on the prisoner.

When his cigar was half-smoked, Rainsford put the brief aside and took off his reading glasses. He was a tall, slender man pushing sixty, yet his hair was unsalted with gray and his eyes were as piercing as ever. Rainsford had learned his law the hard way, reading it in the bunkhouse and finally passing his bar examinations. Years before the bench and on it had sharpened him, and his reputation for firmness was far-reaching.

Rainsford said, "I've never heard of a man being held on this kind of evidence, Eiler." He frowned slightly. "You have an identification of the man. Normally he would have been turned loose."

"Yes, sir, normally he would have," Eiler said. "However, for two reasons this isn't a normal case. First, Price Shatlock was murdered. The State of Texas demands some action there. Secondly, the alternate identity, and you must admit that this is possible, is that of Tass Creel, a professional murderer if there ever was one."

"Very well, we'll give this whole thing a complete and impartial hearing." He leaned back in his chair and took his cigar out of his mouth. "I'd like to talk to the arresting officers."

"I'm sorry, your honor, but they're both off the post on duty." Eiler folded and unfolded his hands. "As you can see from my brief, I've done considerable checking on Moss McKitrick. War Department has no record of him ever having served in the Union forces, yet the surgeon, who gave him a physical examination on my orders, reports an old bullet wound in the thigh."

"A physical?" Rainsford asked.

"Yes, sir. We know that Tass Creel was in the Union army, a sniper. He learned his trade there. As you can see by the attached telegrams, this was verified. He served a year with the Ohio Volunteers, then was mustered out in 1865. Reason: a wound that didn't heal properly."

"In the thigh?" Rainsford asked.

"We don't know, your honor. Records then were sketchy. We can only verify that Creel was a soldier and was discharged because of his wound."

"But hardly in the thigh," Rainsford said. "Good Lord, I've been shot twice, and in worse places, and I'm functioning."

"Yes, sir, and I won't argue the inconclusiveness of this. But Creel is a man shrouded in mystery. So is Moss McKitrick."

Rainsford laughed. "The inscrutable man, eh? Well, we'll see tomorrow morning. I suppose McKitrick has someone on the way here who can positively identify him?"

"The sheriff, Owen Henry. McKitrick's wife is also arriving."

"That'll be a jolly family reunion," Rainsford said. "Sort of a prelude to a civil suit filed in the State of Kansas when he gets home. As an attorney, Eiler, you know what a posture this places us in."

"It is your privilege to dismiss the prisoner," Eiler pointed out.

"And have half the influential friends of Shatlock after my scalp?" He shook his head. "We'll open the ball at ten o'clock, in your office."

"That'll be a little crowded, sir. I suggest the mess tent."

"A tent? Very well. I suppose the public is invited."

"Unless you want a closed hearing," Eiler said.

Rainsford shook his head. "We're in deep enough now. No, let the public in on this. I suppose the damned newspapers—"

"Naturally," Eiler said.

"Naturally," Rainsford echoed, feeling progressively unhappier. He puffed on his cigar a bit longer, then got up and mentioned having had a long day, and this was hint enough; Eiler showed him to his room and then went to the parlor where his wife sat alone.

Eiler sighed as he sat down and his wife looked at him. "You worry too much, Nathan. It never does any good and you know it." She was a slender woman, thirty-some, with dark eyes and hair.

"It's been eight days since Burke Pine left the post," Eiler said. "And no word from him. Six since Cannon left and nothing from him either, except that he's been to Ashland, Kansas, and the last telegram I got was from Medicine Bow, Wyoming." He sighed again and stretched his legs. Someone knocked on his front door and he got up and went to see who it was.

A lanky Texas Ranger stood there, hat in hand. "Sorry to bother you, captain, but we got a wire that Mrs. McKitrick and the sheriff missed train connections this afternoon, so they're coming in by buggy."

"Some time tonight?"

"Yes, sir. Are you comin' back to the post?"

"Yes, damn it," Eiler said. "Thanks, Wylie." He closed the door and went back to the parlor to tell his wife, then he got his coat and his pistol from the hall closet and dropped it into his pocket on the way out.

The sergeant of the guard had the lights on in headquarters when he dismounted; Eiler went directly to his office and a moment later the sergeant of the guard came in. Eiler said, "As soon as Sheriff Henry and Mrs. McKitrick arrive on the post, have them brought here to my office. Send someone into town to make sure they both have hotel accommodations, and put a fresh team and an ambulance at their disposal, along with a driver."

"Ain't that kind of overdoin' it, captain?"

"Sanderson, it just may be that we will need any small kindness they can remember about us. Have the corporal of the guard stand by in the event they want to see McKitrick tonight. In that case, bring him here."

"All right, captain. But he's being treated better than anyone I've ever seen in the guardhouse."

"Has he been behaving himself?"

"No complaints there. He sleeps, reads his Bible, and gives nobody any trouble. Fact is, he acts like a man who's just waitin' to get out."

"That may be closer to the truth than we know," Eiler said.

A newspaperman from Dallas came to the post a half hour later, and Eiler's first impulse was to not see him at all, then he realized that the man must have already been to his home and disturbed his wife, so Eiler had him brought in.

"I'm Fred Sheridan, *Dallas Star.*" He offered his hand and Eiler took it, then Sheridan sat down and crossed his long legs. "A week ago I heard the rumor that two of your men had crossed the border and brought back a man who might be Tass Creel. I just got in town late this evening after riding forty miles from that freight junction south of here. Would you like to fill me in, captain?"

"Mr. Sheridan, I could stand some filling in myself." He explained the question of the prisoner's true identity, emphasizing the necessity of proceeding slowly and carefully so as not to make a legally embarrassing mistake.

When he finished, Fred Sheridan said, "Captain, I take it you're not a reader of the *Dallas Star.*"

"I've read it from time to time," Eiler admitted. "What's your point?"

"Just that everyone in Texas didn't think that Price Shatlock was a great man," Sheridan said, his manner frank. "I've been fourteen years on the *Star.* Inherited my job from a man you never heard of. He started on Shatlock when he and the old power combine began scaring Wyoming farmers into moving out so the country could be turned into rangeland. He was just one small, lonely voice crying out for justice but it was a voice Price Shatlock had to have silenced. That was done with a .45 caliber rifle bullet fired one evening over an incredible distance. Does the method suggest any one man?"

"Tass Creel," Eiler said.

"That was my first feature story," Sheridan said, "the obituary of a man I loved and admired. I wrote other stories over the period of the next year. Some got published. Some didn't because I couldn't prove them and the paper didn't want a suit on its hands." He stood up and took off his coat, unbuttoned his vest, loosened his tie and opened his shirt to expose a terrible scar on his shoulder muscle near the neck. "I'm the only man Tass Creel ever shot at and missed, captain. He caught me getting on a railroad coach at Wichita Falls. That was a long time ago, but it was enough to make certain my interest in Price Shatlock and Tass Creel never diminished even though I never actually saw Creel." He put his clothes back in order and sat down again. "I was in Rock Springs to cover Price Shatlock's hearing, and I stood ten yards away when Creel blew his brains all over the courthouse steps. So you might conclude that my interest in this is more than academic."

"I guess it is," Eiler said. "You are a man of distinction, Mr. Sheridan, having by inches escaped Tass Creel's lethal bullet."

"My two suitcases are at the hotel," Sheridan said, "but I only brought along a spare shirt and some clean collars. The rest is filled with newspaper clippings, from the *Dallas Star*, and other papers. You might like to go over them, captain, for when a man goes to reach far back, there's nothing like a newspaper to help him."

"You may do us a great service," Eiler said. "Yes, I would like to look at them." The sergeant of the guard knocked, then came in.

"Buggy just rolled through the gate, captain. Shall I bring 'em right in?"

"Yes," Eiler said. "Mr. Sheridan, would you mind leaving by the side door? I'll join you there in a few minutes."

He nodded and left, then the sergeant came in, opening the door for a portly man wearing a dusty coat, and a plump woman whose eyes were red from dust irritation.

"Owen Henry," the man said, shaking hands briefly. "This is Mrs. McKitrick. I suppose there'll be a lot of red tape before we can see Moss."

"On the contrary," Eiler said. "I'm having him brought here. And I'm sorry you had such a long and tiring trip."

"To hell with that," Henry said bruskly. "We only want to identify him and get his release."

"I hope that's the case," Eiler said.

"It sure as hell better be," Henry said, then turned as the door opened and Moss McKitrick stepped inside. His wife ran to him and cried and embraced him and he stood there with his stocky arms around her, talking softly, soothingly to her.

Eiler said, "Suppose we step outside, sheriff." He took Henry by the arm and opened the side door.

When it closed, Moss McKitrick loosened his grip on his wife and stepped back a bit from her. "How are the boys?"

"Worried about you," she said. "Moss, what's happened?"

"A mistake," he said. "It made me mad at first, but now I know it's just one of those things that now and then happen to a man."

"But to you, Moss, a man who's never done anyone harm in his life."

He smiled and patted her arm. "Now, Clara, don't get yourself worked up. We'll be goin' home soon and it'll all blow over."

Her manner turned peckish. "I don't see why you had to go hunting anyway. Didn't I tell you it was a foolish thing to do? I said that a hundred times, didn't I, Moss?"

"At least a hundred times," McKitrick said, a touch of resignation coming into his voice.

"It's a foolish thing, going hunting," she said. "Wasteful, that's what it is. You never bring back anything."

"What does it matter now?" he said gently. "Pull yourself together, Clara." He put his arms around her and held her face against his chest and then his eyes turned hard for an instant and darted

55

to both doors as though he were measuring his chances. Then the expression was erased, and Captain Nathan Eiler stepped back inside.

"That's all for now, Mr. McKitrick. You'll see her again in the morning." He saw the tears, the stricken look and knew that she was going to kick her heels and yell, so he had the sergeant take McKitrick out right away, then he called Owen Henry in and told him about the arrangements he had made for them at the hotel.

After they had gone, Fred Sheridan stepped back into the office and closed the side door. He said, "We were both looking through the window, captain. Did you see what I saw?"

"Yes, but what does it really mean? A man turned desperate for a moment? A man fighting to retain his control?" He shook his head. "It's going to take more than the look we saw on his face to change much."

"I wonder if he'd know me now, after these many years?" Sheridan asked. "Creel never made a mistake, you know. He knew the men he went after."

Chapter Four

The day was unusually hot, one of those smoldering, breezeless days which made flies bite, and men fretful and impatient for the change in weather all these symptoms promised.

The mess tent was cleared at eight o'clock and at ten Judge Rainsford opened the hearing. Eiler was there, and Owen Henry and McKitrick and his wife; two rangers stood outside. Fred Sheridan came in after they were all seated and sat in the back, directly behind Moss McKitrick where he couldn't readily be seen unless McKitrick deliberately turned around and looked.

Judge Rainsford said, "This is not a trial, and there is no accused; no charges of any kind are being brought. Our fuction here is to hold a hearing for the purpose of establishing identity. Normally, this hearing would not be necessary, but the nature and character of the identity in question is of sufficient importance to warrant care that no mistake is ever made. Let it be clear that we are as dedicated to proving Mr. McKitrick's identity beyond the shadow of doubt, as we are to establishing a clearer picture of Tass Creel. This hearing will serve two purposes: One, if Mr. McKitrick *is* Mr. McKitrick, of Ashland, Kansas, we will forever remove him from the possibility of being confused again, and: Two, we will provide to law enforcement officers in Texas a clearer image of the man they want." He glanced at Sheriff Owen Henry. "Would you please step forward and sit in this chair by my table? Thank you. You wouldn't mind answering a few questions?"

"I'll answer anything you want to ask me," Henry said confidently.

"How long have you been the sheriff at Ashland?"

Henry thought a moment. "Twelve years come September. I was there two years before I ran for office. And I've known Moss McKitrick all that time."

"We'll get to that," Rainsford said, his tone chiding. "Are you familiar with the name: Tass Creel?"

"Never heard of it," Owen Henry said frankly. "I run a tidy office and I've never seen a dodger on Creel. Never had any communication from any other law officer either about him." He shifted in his chair and crossed his legs. "The first I heard the name was in connection with this mess."

"I see," Rainsford said. "Then you are prepared to identify Moss McKitrick as a resident of Ashland?"

"Certainly am," Henry said. He smiled at McKitrick as though to assure him that this would all be over in a few minutes. A ranger stepped into the tent and touched Captain Nathan Eiler on the shoulder and handed him a telegram. Eiler read it, then passed it back to Fred Sheridan to read.

Rainsford, observing this, said, "Is this a matter concerning us, captain?"

"Yes, judge. May I approach the bench?" Rainsford nodded and Eiler came up with the telegram. Rainsford opened it and read: *Hold up the show. Returning on night train with man who knows Creel. Pine.*

Rainsford returned the telegram, then said, "I would like to declare a five-minute recess. Captain, if I might have a word with you." He left his chair and stepped to the far corner of the mess tent and spoke softly. "I know Pine by reputation so I wouldn't question the sincerity of his message. But with Owen Henry's identification of McKitrick, how can I reasonably hold the man more than another hour?"

"I'd like to question Henry. Will you grant me some latitude if I seem to wander afar?"

Rainsford nodded, but he was frowning. "We're tottering on the edge of a civil suit that we can't win, Nathan. Be careful."

"I'm aware of the implications," Eiler said. "Still, I want Burke Pine's man to have a look at McKitrick."

Rainsford sighed. "Very well. But it's dangerous."

He returned to the table and the hearing was

reopened. "Captain Eiler, do you have any questions to address to Sheriff Henry?"

"Thank you, judge; I have." He got up and stood before Henry and it was a moment before he spoke. "You've known McKitrick for fourteen years. That's a long time. You must know a great deal about him."

"I do," Henry said.

"McKitrick is a prosperous man, I understand."

"He's better than average well fixed," Henry said.

"When he goes hunting each year, how long does he stay away from Ashland?"

"What?" Henry frowned. "Two months. Yes, about that."

"I see. And of course he goes about the same time each year?"

"Well," Henry said, scratching his head, "I really couldn't say."

"Why not?"

"Because I don't keep that close watch on people. No reason to. If a man wants to leave town for awhile, then I figure it's his business."

"A sensible attitude to take," Eiler said pleasantly. "What did you do before you became sheriff?"

"I had a ranch. Lost it. Cattle got anthrax." Henry frowned. "What the hell are you getting at?"

"I'm only trying to know you better," Eiler said. "Where did McKitrick usually go to hunt?"

"Never asked him."

"Must have been far to be gone two months. Perhaps into the Rockies for sheep? Or Alaska or Canada for bear? What type of game did McKitrick bring back?"

"I never said he brought any back," Henry said.

"He hunted for trophies then? Heads to be mounted on the wall?"

Henry shrugged. "I don't go snooping around his house."

"All right, we'll let that pass. McKitrick is an excellent shot, then?"

"He never carried a gun as long as I've known him," Henry said.

Eiler turned quickly and snapped his fingers, drawing the attention of the guards. "Case, bring in the rifle out of my office." He turned back and looked at Owen Henry. "When McKitrick was taken into custody he had in his possession a long-barreled sniper's Springfield. When the guard returns with it, I would like to have you identify it."

"If I can," Henry said. The guard came into the tent and Eiler took the rifle and turned it over in his hands so that Henry got a good look. The sheriff shook his head. "Never saw it before." He looked at McKitrick. "Where'd you get that, Moss?"

"I bought it from a man on the train," McKitrick said. "We were stopping at Amarillo and he wanted a drink. He sold me the rifle for eight dollars."

"Eight dollars?" Eiler asked. "This gun must be worth sixty dollars in any kind of a market."

"I know a bargain when I see one," McKitrick said. "That's why I bought it, figuring to sell it later to some wolfer and pay for my trip."

"And the ammunition?" Eiler asked.

"The fella gave me some shells," McKitrick said. "What good would they do him without the rifle?" He leaned back in his chair. "How long is this nonsense goin' on anyway?"

"To me it is not nonsense," Eiler said. "All right, sheriff, you can take your seat now." Henry started to get up, then Eiler startled him by changing his mind, by pushing him back into the chair. "A few more questions, sheriff. McKitrick is a farmer?"

"That's right."

"A good one?"

"Well—yes."

"You hesitated. Why?"

"Well, I don't know as it's my place to say."

Rainsford said, "Just answer the question, sheriff. You said you'd answer—"

"All right, all right," Henry said, waving his hand. He looked at Nathan Eiler. "To tell the truth, Moss never struck any of us as being much of a farmer. He wasn't lazy, but it just seemed that he couldn't quite take care of a place. You know."

"No, I don't know," Eiler said. "Tell me."

Henry seemed uncomfortable; he glanced at McKitrick as though apologizing. "Moss, he never did have the knack a farmer needs, if you know what I mean. He'd buy hogs when they was high and sell when they were low, and he just couldn't put pounds on an animal. He'd take a notion to skimp on feed when it was cheap, then hand feed when it was high." Henry shook his head and chuckled. "Danged if it didn't worry some of us, because a man can go under if he ain't careful."

"But he made out all right," Eiler said, looking at McKitrick. "You told me yourself that he was well off."

"It's true," Henry said. "Somehow Moss always comes out, shows a profit, and has a little to put by. But he has a canny way with money, I guess."

"You're contradicting yourself," Eiler pointed out. "On one hand you tell me he is a foolish spender and on the other you tell me he is cagey. Now which is it?"

"Maybe both," Henry said, "if that's possible. When a place came up for sale, Moss managed to come up with the money to buy." He turned in the chair and looked at Judge Rainsford. "Should I be talkin' about these things I don't rightly know all about?"

"The questioning seems fair under the

circumstances," Rainsford said. He looked at his watch. "I think, in view of the nearness of noon, we might postpone the hearing." He took out a handkerchief and wiped sweat from his face. "If this heat keeps up, I see no sense in roasting in here this afternoon. We'll meet in the morning and hope it's cooler."

Moss McKitrick frowned. "What's the sense in dragging this out?" He got up and faced Eiler. "I know something about law, captain. Charge me or let me go on home with my wife."

Rainsford spoke softly. "Nathan, you really can't hold him longer without charge. I'm sorry. The man has his rights."

"Very well," Eiler said firmly. "I'll have a complaint on your desk in an hour, charging him with firing on two peace officers in the discharge of their duty."

"That was in Mexico," McKitrick snapped. "You've got no legal grounds—"

"The arresting officers are absent from the post," Eiler said, "and I'd have to check that with them when they return. I think the charge will stick, judge."

"Mmm," Rainsford said, brushing his thick mustache. "At least until the officers return. You may take the prisoner to his confinement now."

A nod brought the guards in and McKitrick was taken out. Owen Henry remained with McKitrick's wife. He said, "This is the damnest state I ever been in and once I'm out of it I'm never coming back." He went over to Eiler and took him by the arm and turned him around. "You just can't get it through your head that you've got an innocent man, can you?"

"If you mean, am I convinced of his innocence, I'd have to say no. Henry, you're not a stupid man. Surely you can see the holes in McKitrick's story."

"Oh, you're a terrible man, saying a thing like that about Moss," Mrs. McKitrick snapped. She puckered her lips in distaste and looked on the verge of tears.

"This is unpleasant," Eiler said, "but we will get at the truth."

"I already know the truth," she said. "He's a kind, loving man." She lifted the hem of her dress and flounced out.

Owen Henry said, "She was always easy to upset. An Ashland girl. She's been a good wife to Moss. Not one of those women who keeps a man on edge all the time, rollin' their eyes at fellas on the street. But she's been a good woman. Never been a trouble to Moss."

"Some women barely miss being an old maid," Eiler said. "How close did she come?"

Henry was surprised. Then he laughed. "You're no fool, I can see. Well, I guess Moss was her first and last offer. She was always a little heavy, and some said her tongue was a little sharp. I guess

65

that's so. Moss courted her a spell—before my time in town—and they've made a go of it."

"A woman who's overweight and has a sharp tongue must have had something to offer a man," Eiler said.

Henry nodded. "Always pokin', ain't you? Got to make somethin' out of everything, don't you? Well, there wasn't nothing."

"Absolutely nothing?" Eiler smiled. "Or is it because you don't want to say and make me out right?"

He was getting to Owen Henry and the sheriff squirmed. "She had this house in town. Folks left it to her. And there was the farm. Not much. Ninety acres or so." He took off his hat and wiped away the sweat in the band. "All right, you made your point, but it don't change my mind about Moss McKitrick."

He turned then and went out, and Fred Sheridan got up and came over. "You know how to ride a man, captain. He's honest—Henry, I mean. Not too smart, but honest. If you worked on him and he knew anything at all, you'd get it out of him."

"Did McKitrick see you today?"

Sheridan shook his head. "When he got up to turn, I bent way over and made out I was fussing with my shoe. He passed by me without a glance."

Eiler thought about this. "Tomorrow, when we have a man here who actually saw Tass Creel, I think I can break that shell McKitrick wears. If he opens up the smallest crack, I want you to come forward and let him look at you. Creel would know you and I'll be watching for any sign of recognition."

"All right," Sheridan said. "You're convinced he's Creel?"

"It's a feeling in my bones," Eiler said and left the tent.

Rainsford had his evening meal in Nathan Eiler's office; there wasn't much talk until they poured the coffee and lit cigars, then Rainsford said, "It's my judicial opinion, Nathan, that you had better not test the validity of McKitrick's arrest in Mexico. By that, I mean if Burke Pine doesn't come in a ringer, you'll turn him loose."

"I'm taking that as an order," Eiler said.

Rainsford smiled. "It's my hope that you'll take it as a suggestion from a man who thinks you're doing a tough job very well. I wouldn't want to have to make it an order from the bench, but I will if this goes too far."

"Judge, if this man is Creel, and he's released, we'll never find him again. Any man who can stay shrouded in mystery so many years is bound to disappear completely."

"If this man is Creel, he won't be released."

The cook came and took away their trays, then the sergeant of the guard came in with a telegram. Eiler ripped it open.

Eiler passed the telegram over for Rainsford's inspection, then the judge said, "A man who knew Creel and a man who spoke to him. I hope to God they take a look at the prisoner and say they never saw him before. Be rid of this mess for good, then."

"You would, sir. I wouldn't, for I'd still want the man."

Rainsford closed his eyes and puffed on his cigar. "Eighteen eighty-seven, that's a long time ago. Where has this man been, Eiler? Why hasn't he come forward?"

"They never do, judge. They walk the streets and move from place to place with their secrets, and then someone, or something, forces them to talk. Shatlock was going to talk. I don't suppose we ever will find out what made him offer a confession." He flicked cigar ash in a glass tray on his desk. "I've broken a few cases that were ten or fifteen years old. Sometimes it is easier than solving a newer crime because time makes some men relax, makes the truth easier to pry out. Then too there is always the unexpected deathbed confession that breaks a dam loose and brings out facts hidden for years." He got up and went to the door and spoke to the guard in the yard. "As soon as Pine shows up—"

"We'll shoo him right in, cap'n," the man said and went on walking his post.

Eiler came back and sat down. His cigar was a sour butt and he started to take a final pull on it, glanced at it, and butted it out.

Rainsford said, "I recall the Kyle Dixon case now. He was riding in his buggy with his son and was bushwhacked. The son escaped or was made off with, for he was never found."

"Since this affair has come up," Eiler said, "I've suspected that Charlie Dixon was alive. Judge, when a man dies, there's a body. They combed the country for the boy and found nothing. Dixon was a leader of his faction. His friends wouldn't let this rest until they'd exhausted all possibilities. No, I'm convinced the boy got away and now— well, who knows about now."

A buggy came into the yard, and a moment later Burke Pine stepped into the office with a tall, tree-straight man in his late sixties. Pine said, "Captain, I'd like you to meet Colonel Lavery, U. S. Army."

"Retired, sir," Lavery said and presented his left

hand for shaking since the right arm had been amputated at the shoulder.

Eiler introduced Judge Rainsford, then walked over and closed the door. He came back, waved them into chairs, then sat down. "Perhaps you'd like to tell me, colonel—in your own way—what you know of Tass Creel."

"It's been years since I've heard that name." He smiled thinly. "Years since I thought of him, and when I did, I always wondered what tree he was hung from. The man was doomed for it, you know. But we took all kinds during the Rebellion."

"Would you recognize Creel now, sir?" Rainsford asked.

Colonel Lavery frowned. "Sir, you're asking me to span nearly thirty years, and my eyes aren't what they used to be either. Creel came to my attention in the early spring of 1865. Grant was trying to take Richmond from the south and we'd laid siege to Petersburg. Perhaps you recall the event, sir."

"Yes," Rainsford said. "Nearly a year, wasn't it?"

Lavery nodded. "We were bogged down. The troops were dug in, setting up housekeeping. Getting them to move presented a problem. Once men are set, they resist a change." He took out a handkerchief and wiped his forehead.

Eiler said, "Colonel, can I offer you a drink?"

"Thank you. It might pick me up." He smiled. "Sergeant Pine likes to cover ground and my health has been marginal." He took the glass Eiler offered and tossed it down. Immediately color came into his face, and he sighed deeply. "That's better. Builds a little fire in a man's gut. I've been retired for twelve years now. Lost my arm in the Apache campaigns."

Judge Rainsford looked at Burke Pine and said, "Would you mind telling me how you located Colonel Lavery?"

"Just used the old noodle, judge."

"That's enough bragging," Eiler said. "Let's have the facts."

Pine smiled for he was enjoying this. "Well, I figured I'd better start somewhere, and the beginning seemed logical. Then I asked myself who kept records of everything. The answer was simple: the Army. So since the State of Texas was payin' for it, I took the train to Fort Leavenworth, Kansas, and let the adjutant look it up for me. I found out who Creel's commanding officer was, and that he was dead. Colonel Lavery's name came up twice. I got his location and went there."

Eiler nodded. "Colonel, it was good of you to come here."

"I must confess that I didn't make the trip merely to see any ends of justice served," Lavery said. "Creel himself is fascination enough to pull any man away from the comforts of retirement."

He took out a cigar case and Pine hurriedly cracked a match into flame. Lavery smiled around his puffing, and said, "You'd make an excellent orderly, sergeant. I suppose you saw your service on the other side?"

"Three years in the cavalry," Pine said.

Rainsford said, "Go on with your story, colonel."

"Of course," Lavery said. "I was a captain then, brevet colonel, with regimental duties." He leaned back in his chair and held his cigar loosely between his fingers. "War takes on a strange complexion when you are immobilized by the enemy or by the terrain, or the other facets of war. Virginia is beautiful, or it must have been before the scars of war had been inflicted on her. To us she was a shocked, disturbed, molested, and faintly hostile, mistrusted thing. We ate off her land, polluted her streams, consorted with her women, all with the notion of moving on and leaving her vastly worse than we'd found her."

"And Creel?" Eiler asked.

Lavery shrugged. "A private. Company duties, I suppose, and from what I gather, badly performed. Much of him I learned through reports and conversation with his commanding officer and sergeants. He was—if I can make myself clear—a man incapable of doing anything completely right. Except killing, of course. His record as a sniper was excellent, and that was about the only type of action going on, you know. Our most forward positions could see into the town, and our snipers watched for targets. Creel would have been most happy, I'm sure, to have lived in a tree, forever looking for a target. But it wasn't all that way. He made a miserable soldier. Even mess duty seemed beyond his capabilities, and he caught it often for failure to come to the mark, or for some minor infraction of discipline." Lavery paused to enjoy his cigar. "In talking with him, I got the impression that he felt put upon because in his mind his sole role, his complete function, was to kill, and other than care for his weapon, he was useless, most unreliable." He laid his cigar aside, and his voice turned soft and his mind rolled aside the years and a total recall returned. "We loved the land and we hated it because we were forced to occupy it and it was not ours. All that lush green land with the rains falling nearly every afternoon and afterward the steam rising from the fields, and it was not ours at all, for somehow men want a particular place, need it, must have it, and are totally dissatisfied with any other. Can you see this, gentlemen? Stationary for nearly a year, wanting battle, dreading it, wanting a change, loathing the thought of it. There was no worse place on earth, no set of circumstances more undesirable than this. And then you have a man like Tass Creel . . ."

Chapter Five

He killed the officer and he felt good because it had been a long shot, perhaps the longest he had ever made, and the light had been poor, near sundown with the strong sunlight slanting heavy through the trees lining the distant street.

It was good to think of that shot, for he had waited all the day with nothing worth firing on. Then this officer had come to the porch to stand and look at the quiet town. It had been very quiet. The sounds of insects made a whirring and on the other side of town, a milk cow lowed and he could hear it clearly. He watched the officer and silently urged him to step onto the walk, to approach the edge of the street where a clear shot would be possible.

The range; he knew it exactly: six hundred and seventy-five yards, and the wind was a breeze blowing gently at his back. It raised a sweat on his face, this silent urging for the officer to step to the street, and finally he did, standing at the curb edge as though waiting for a carriage to come up and stop.

He braced the rifle, made the last minute adjustment on the sight and settled his breathing. Then he cocked the piece, keeping his finger away from the set trigger; a breath would discharge it, and he had to be sure. His target was minute even in the magnified power of the long telescope and when he was satisfied, the tip of his finger touched the trigger and the piece roared and booted his shoulder and he lowered the gun and sat there, waiting.

He could hear the thwack of the bullet when it hit the officer and he watched the man clap both hands to his breast, stagger, and fall, calling out as he went down.

People started to run out of their houses, then they stopped, afraid they would be killed, and he watched them hang back while the officer thrashed about in the street, beyond help.

It took him nearly ten minutes to die, then Tass Creel climbed down out of the tree and went down the narrow, rutted road to his company. As he walked to his tent, he met the sergeant, who stopped him.

"I heard a shot," the sergeant said. He was a tall, muscular man with a swarthy face and cool gray eyes, and when he spoke to Creel, he looked down because Creel was short and slight, a man with little more than down on his face.

"It was too far away to tell what his rank was," Creel said. "But I killed him. The best shot I ever made. The longest. I heard the bullet hit him."

"I'll tell the captain," the sergeant said and hurried on like he couldn't bear to be around any longer. Creel watched him go and he didn't get angry because he was feeling fine now, feeling proud because he had done his job.

In the center of the camp was a notice board and he stopped to read it and saw his name down for night guard and he went on, dismissing it from his mind as a mistake; he'd done his work and they wouldn't want him to do anything else now.

He was so sure of this that he changed his shirt and left the camp and followed the creek for two miles. The army was everywhere, yet he could not think of this as war; they were in the midst of rebel farm country, surrounded by rebels, yet it was not war. Rather it was an excursion, an excuse to kill when the opportunity presented itself and not be condemned for it.

War—his notion of war—was masses of troops fighting and noise and clouds of powdersmoke and dust, not a walk along the creek in country now as familiar to him as his own Iowa.

His destination was the Bricker farm; he went there often, even after he had been forbidden to go there, and he would go back because he always felt a deep dissatisfaction after his visits. There was an old man, and an old woman, grandparents, and the girl, young, in her mid-teens, and he could never understand how she felt about him.

Creel was not sure how he felt about her, but that didn't matter. It never mattered how he felt toward anyone, for he measured everything the other way, how he felt about things. He hated the sergeant and the company commander, a thin, nasal-speaking man from Vermont, and he was getting to hate all the corporals because they were always picking on him, always giving him duty and he didn't need anyone to tell him his duty because he knew it and did it better than anyone in the regiment. They'd be talking about that shot he made this afternoon for a week.

The Bricker girl's name was Jennie and he had spent a lot of time with her, and it was good and it was bad. Good because he could talk to her, and bad because all the talk never settled anything and always led him back to talk some more.

She met him in a field near some hay ricks and they walked back toward the creek. He thought her pretty, and she was, in a big-boned way. The southern women were having a tough time of it, but Jennie managed to keep food on the table and some decent clothes on her back and Creel knew that the sergeant and a couple of the corporals brought her things and he wondered what they got in return, although he had never asked.

He brought her nothing, and it never occurred to him to bring her anything, for he wasn't a man who gave, only took. As they walked across the field, he tried to take her hand but she pulled it away.

"Why'd you do that?" he asked.

"I just wanted to, that's all," she said.

He said, "Did you ever swim in the creek? There's a good swimmin' hole a ways up."

"Sometimes I do," she said.

"Why don't we go now?"

She looked at him and laughed. "Why, I wouldn't go in there with a boy."

"Who do you go with then?" Creel asked.

"I go by myself, that's who."

He walked on a short way. "You ain't afraid to take your clothes off, are you?" He put his eyes on her, boldly, challenging her. Color came to her cheeks and he kept looking at her and he knew she had and it drove a fire through him. "I'll bet you and the sergeant go there."

A flame of anger came into her eyes, but it never touched him. Grass rustled near her feet and she looked down, then screeched and jumped back as a young bull snake slithered off through the grass.

Creel bounded after it, caught it, and brought it back, writhing and trying to get free and she backed away, fear in her eyes. She never thought he'd really come near her with it, and she held her ground, and when she realized what he was going to do, it was too late to run.

He grabbed her, threw her down while she screamed, and he sat on her and pushed the bull snake down the front of her dress, then got up.

She went into a wild, fearful dance, all the while ripping away her clothes. Her dress, petticoats, shift were torn away from her until the snake was free. Creel watched her, watched the glassy-eyed, stretched-mouth fear, then she started running across the field, leaving her clothes behind her.

He waited until she was far away, then he turned and went back to his company and laid down in his tent to sleep. The sergeant found him there and booted him awake.

"Damn it, you're on guard duty, Creel. Get up."

He took his time about it and reported to the corporal and was given an issue carbine and he marched up and down for two hours, the weapon on his shoulder, and finally he was relieved and went over to the mess tent for some coffee.

While he was there drinking it, the sergeant found him and took him by the arm and led him out. "I want to talk to you."

He had to go along because the sergeant was burly and he was slight and the sergeant took him away from the tent to a grove of trees and there he pushed Creel against a big bole and banged his head against the bark a few times.

"I ought to kill you now," the sergeant said. "Give me one reason not to."

"You're hurtin' my head," Creel said. "I didn't hurt her none. If she says I did, then she's a liar."

The sergeant knew that talk was no good, that it would never be any good, so he started hitting Creel with his big, burly fists, and Creel didn't fight back much; he just let the sergeant open up the cuts on his face and he bled for him and it satisfied the sergeant and he let him go.

After the sergeant left, Tass Creel sat down under the tree and felt proud of himself for he hadn't cried out when he'd been hit, and he'd stood up to the sergeant. His lip was cut and there was another on his cheekbone, and his left eye would be swollen shut in the morning, but he didn't care because it wasn't his shooting eye.

He went back to camp and his tent and blankets but he couldn't sleep, and for many weeks following he didn't sleep well because even after his cuts healed he'd lay there and think of the sergeant and feel the burly fists against his face and all this thinking was a fester in his bowels and he couldn't get rid of it.

His habits of living did not change. He did his duty in a careless manner and twice went before the captain for a dressing down, and once before the regimental commander, a stern-faced man who had no pity at all, no memory of the good work Tass Creel did with his telescoped sniping rifle. They never remembered that, only that he had spilled the potatoes he had been peeling, or that he was late for guard duty, or failed to bring wood for the cook fires.

In his spare time he went back to the Bricker place and he watched the house, but he never went near it, and he never let himself be seen. He did not find this difficult for he had a natural knack of concealing himself, of being unobtrusive, and he considered it a part of his business.

He did this watching and waiting with no particular plan in mind, but when the opportunity came to him, his instincts told him how right it was, and he acted. The sergeant and the girl went to the creek and walked along it to the swimming hole and while they swam and laughed and played in the water, he made his quiet, unseen approach.

Creel had no gun or knife and he wanted neither; a handy clump of wood would serve him nicely and he waited in the grass near their clothes and finally they came out and sprawled on the blanket the sergeant had brought. Darkness was coming on rapidly now and it suited them and he listened to their talk; she was a different girl now; he did not know her at all, or want to.

The sergeant had his back to Creel; he was sitting up, the girl in his lap, and he never heard Creel at all. The wood thumped against his skull and he fell forward, pinning the girl.

Creel put his hand over her mouth and cut off her cry, and threw the stick in the brush while he fumbled among the sergeant's clothes. He found what he wanted, the neckerchief, and he wound it around Jennie Bricker's throat and tightened it and held her until the life left her.

Then he went back to his tent and slept the night through.

The sergeant reported the murder and was

arrested for it, and as soon as the news passed through the camp that the court-martial would be held, Tass Creel volunteered to testify for the Army.

A lieutenant questioned him at length, and was finally satisfied that his testimony would close the case, and he was made to stand in the sun outside the regimental commander's tent until called in.

The solemn proceedings impressed him, and the sergeant sat with an armed guard on either side of him and he looked steadily at Tass Creel while the oath was administered.

The lieutenant asked the questions; his manner was brisk for the whole thing was distasteful and everyone seemed to want to get it over quickly and go back to the relative decency of war.

"Private Creel, will you relate to the court exactly what you know of this matter?"

"Yes, sir." He paused as though gathering the facts into a concise, logical order. "Several times I've seen the sergeant go to the farm, sir. He's been keeping company with the girl there."

"What were you doing near the farm?" the lieutenant asked.

"On duty, sir, foraging for chickens and wood for the fire. I wouldn't go there without permission, sir."

"Very well. Did you see the accused leave camp on the night of the murder?"

"Yes, sir. Before dark, sir."

"And did you see him return?"

"Yes, sir. Well after dark, but I saw him."

The lieutenant turned to another officer. "You may examine the witness, Mr. Beamish."

"Thank you." Beamish, a young, moon-faced man, approached the witness. "Private Creel, you say that you noticed the sergeant leave and come back. Now I have questioned every man in your company and not one—not one, mind you—saw him both leave and return. Can you explain how you alone saw this?"

"Yes, sir. I saw him leave because he passed down my company street. When he returned, I noticed that he was without a neckerchief. This struck me as odd, sir, because the sergeant is a regular soldier, and a stickler for proper dress."

"Oh, come now," Beamish said. "I never heard that the accused was overly fussy."

"Three times last month I was given punishment for not being in proper dress, sir," Creel said. "From this I assumed that the sergeant was a stickler."

Colonel Lavery, who was the senior officer, said, "I believe he has answered the question, Mr. Beamish. Have you anything further?"

"Yes, sir, I have." He turned to Tass Creel. "It is a medical fact that the accused suffered a blow on the head; the lump was promient enough to be seen at a distance of several feet. Would it seem logical to you that the sergeant would strangle the girl then hit himself on the head?"

Colonel Lavery said, "That's not a proper question, Mr. Beamish."

"With your permission, sir, I'd like to have this man's answer."

"Very well. Answer the question, Private Creel."

"Well, sir, I don't know what happened to the sergeant, but a man can fall in the dark. Some weeks ago I fell and cut my face and blackened an eye." He smiled. "To anyone at first glance, it might have looked like I'd been in a fight. Of course, sir, one look at my knuckles would have proved otherwise."

Beamish turned away and clenched his fists before turning back. "Answer yes or no. Hasn't the accused punished you repeatedly since you've been in this company?"

"Yes, sir."

"And isn't it true that you hate the accused?"

"No, sir. The sergeant was just doing his duty."

Beamish waved his hand; he had all he wanted, and maybe more than he wanted.

The other officer stood up. "May I ask another question on re-direct, sir?" Colonel Lavery nodded and the officer came up to the witness. "Private Creel, you know the sergeant well?"

"How do you mean, sir?"

"I mean, are you familiar with his moods? Can you tell when he is calm or angry or excited?"

"Yes, sir. He cusses, sir."

The officer smiled. "And what mood would you say the accused was in when he came back from the swimming hole?"

"Well, excited, sir. He cussed."

"Repeat what you heard." Creel hesitated and the officer prodded him. "You are not uttering oaths, but repeating them. Tell the court."

"Well, the sergeant was yellin', 'Where the Goddamnhell's the corporal of the guard?' Then he went on and I didn't hear anything else."

"Thank you. That will be all."

Tass Creel left the tent and ate that evening by the squad fire and no one spoke to him or came near him and it didn't bother him a bit. By noon the next day, the verdict had been rendered and he never saw the sergeant again, but a week later he heard a rumor drifting down that he had been hung.

He got a new sergeant, a skinny little man with a whining voice and a driving manner, and the first contact he had with him was a summons to the regimental commander's tent. He checked his uniform and reported and Colonel Lavery was alone.

He looked at Creel a moment, then said, "Sit down, Creel. How do you like your new sergeant?" He waited for an answer and didn't get one, so he shrugged and lit a cigar. "You killed the girl, didn't you?"

Tass Creel looked at him, his expression innocent. "Me, sir? Why would I do that?"

Lavery said, "All right, let it go. A good man is dead. That girl—that child, really—is dead. And the sergeant's wife and family, I suppose the news will get to them somehow; that kind of news always does." He stared at Tass Creel. "I want you to know how many people are going to be hurt, and you're not going to be hurt at all." He flicked ash from his smoke. "You saw the sergeant come and go, is that it?"

"Yes, sir."

"That's unusual. No one recalls seeing you."

"Well, sir, I guess I'm just in the habit of not being seen. I wouldn't live long as a sniper if I showed myself." He smiled. "So I just walk quiet and talk quiet and nobody sees me at all. You might say I'm a fella that don't stand out much. People see me and they really don't see me at all."

"You've got an answer for everything, haven't you?" Lavery asked.

"I guess so, sir. Every time I don't, I get in trouble."

"All right, you may go," Lavery said. He watched Creel get up and turn to the tent entrance, then he spoke again and the man stopped. "Where do you come from? Who are your parents?"

"Ain't that in the record, sir?" He stood there with his innocent-faced insolence, then Lavery waved his hand and Tass Creel went out.

• • •

A cold coffee pot sat on Nathan Eiler's desk and his ashtray was crowded with cigar stubs. He got up and stretched and walked to the window; it was near dawn and the sky was getting light. He turned his head and looked at Paul Lavery. "You've thought about this for a long time, haven't you?"

"And regretted it from start to finish," Lavery said. "We moved too fast. A lot came out later because I wouldn't let it go. The business about the snake I learned from the grandparents. A long and continued questioning by myself and my officers brought to light the fact that some remembered seeing the sergeant with torn knuckles right after the snake incident. Only I drew the connection between that and Creel's 'fall.'" He shook his head sadly. "My only and lasting regret is that I could do nothing to Creel. By the time I had made up my mind what I was going to do, several months had passed. We moved out and shortly after, Creel was hit and hospitalized. Again I'd had a chance to think. The war was moving more rapidly and I couldn't spare the time to pursue it further. So I recommended to the surgeon that Tass Creel be dismissed from the service because of his wound."

Eiler glanced at Judge Rainsford and knew what he was going to ask before he spoke. "Colonel, where was the wound?"

"I'm sorry to say that I don't know," Lavery admitted. "It was not crippling, that I do know."

"Was it in the thigh?" Rainsford asked.

"It's possible. I'm sorry, I can't say positively."

"Be light soon," Burke Pine said. He had his chin touching his chest, sitting slouched in his chair. "A man could look through the guardhouse window right into the cell. Colonel, how about you havin' a look?"

Lavery glanced at Eiler, who nodded, and they all left the office and walked across the parade ground to the guardhouse. The sergeant came around to see what was going on, but left when Eiler spoke softly to him.

There was enough light now to see clearly the man sleeping in the cell and for a full three minutes, Paul Lavery studied the supine man. Then he turned and walked back to Eiler's office without saying anything.

When he got inside, he said, "I really don't know. There's a lot of years behind my recollection. Captain, I'm sorry, but I couldn't swear a man into a hangman's noose unless I was positive."

"Damn it," Burke Pine said softly. Then he snapped his fingers. "Captain, listen to this now. The colonel can't swear that McKitrick is Tass Creel, but he wouldn't know that. Creel would remember you, colonel. Let's march you in at the right time, and let Creel have a look. He may give himself away."

"Maybe," Eiler said. "Better still, let's bring Fred Sheridan in on this. After all, Creel marked him for a killing and missed him. Together it may produce something."

"It's too thin," Judge Rainsford said. "So he breaks? What real proof is that? I'm sorry, gentlemen, but we've got to have more."

"Surely you're not going to release him now?" Eiler asked.

"No, not by a long shot," Rainsford said. "Still, your idea is not all bad, Burke. Colonel, I want to make sure this man does not see you until the proper time. Let's just hope that Cannon brings something a little more solid."

Burke Pine brightened. "Have you heard from that knothead?"

"He's due in today," Eiler said. He took out his watch and glanced at it and winced. "We could get two hours sleep anyway. Hardly seems worth stretching out for, does it?"

"Talk for yourself," Burke Pine said, and sauntered outside.

Chapter Six

Moss McKitrick was allowed some privileges not regularly given to prisoners; he took his meals in his cell, but his wife was allowed to eat with him and the guard always left the outer office and went outside so they could talk.

She was unhappy and fretful and wanted to go home. "Moss, when I get back I'm going to draw the money out of the bank and hire a lawyer and sue these people for what they've done to you." He ate while she talked and it irritated her for she kept putting out her hand and stopping his before the fork got to his mouth. "Do you hear me, Moss?"

"Yes, I hear you," he said. "What good does it do to talk about it now?"

"Well it makes me feel better to talk about it," she said. "Oh, if you only hadn't gone on that silly hunting trip in the first place. Haven't I told you it was a waste of time? What good does it do except to take you away from me? Moss, will you stop eating?"

"I'm hungry," he said. "Drink your coffee, Clara."

"It gives me heartburn." She put her hand on his arm again. "Moss, will you pay attention to me?"

"God, what do you want me to do, Clara?" He

raised his voice and she reared back a bit and tears formed in her eyes.

"You know I never liked for you to shout," she said. "Why do you want to hurt me, Moss?"

"Everything I say, everything I do, you think it's something done to hurt you," he said. "Clara, do you have to be persecuted to be happy?"

She stood up, dabbing at her eyes. "I'm going to leave you now, Moss, and when you're not angry at me, I'll come back. I love you and I'll stick by you."

His tone hardened as though he were holding on to his patience. "Clara, will you stop this? I'm not mad at you. There's no need to go."

"I know best," she said. "I've lived with you long enough to know."

She rattled the cell door and the guard let her out and she walked across the parade ground, sniffing and crying to herself. The guard on the headquarters porch stopped her before she could go in.

"I want to see the captain," she said.

"He's sleepin', ma'am."

"But I must talk to him."

He shrugged and went inside and a few minutes later he came out and opened the door for her. When she stepped into Eiler's office she found him washing his face. He waved her into a chair, towelled dry, then sat down.

"How can I help you, Mrs. McKitrick?"

"I've just got to have somebody to talk to," she said. "I feel so lost, so alone here. I'm used to my home. This is my first trip away."

"Really," Eiler said. "Do you mind if I smoke?"

"Oh, no, you go right ahead." She folded and unfolded her hands. "Moss, he never liked to have me go much. A woman's place is in her home, he always said, and Moss knows best. We have two boys, you know. Two fine boys. Wyley and Burgess. Moss adores them." She laughed shyly. "If Sheriff Henry hadn't come with me, I don't know as I'd have dared make the trip."

"Everyone should travel a bit," Eiler said. "Last year my wife and I went to San Francisco for a month. Had a wonderful time."

"Did you see oranges on the trees?" she asked. "I saw a picture of an orchard of orange trees and I always wanted to pick one and eat it."

He laughed softly. "Yes, we picked some oranges. Mrs. McKitrick, when this business is ended, why don't you and your husband go on a trip somewhere? Chicago maybe, or New Orleans. It wouldn't cost much."

"I don't think Moss would want me to go," she said. "He has his own ideas, you know, and he's not a man to argue with."

He sat there for a minute, watching her, gauging her. Then he said, "Shouldn't you be having breakfast with your husband? Mrs. McKitrick, have you and your husband had a quarrel?"

The button was there to be pressed and he released the dam of tears and a torrent of words.

"He puts me off somehow," she wailed. "He was always a reserved man, inclined to be silent, and when we were courtin' I drew strength from that. It's because I'd been sheltered all my life, and I couldn't stand a coarse man." She wiped her eyes and blew her nose. "The first year or so I was happy because Moss wasn't a demanding husband, yet it bothered me, this coolness, as though he sometimes pushed me away. I love that man; he's all I've got. But I wanted to be needed. Do you understand that? He's got to need me."

"I'm sure he needs you," Eiler said.

She shook her head. "No he don't. I've come here to him, like a proper wife should, but he acts as though he wishes I'd stayed home and left him alone."

"He's under a nervous strain," Eiler said. "You can't expect him to be thinking of much of anything except getting out and going home."

"Do you really mean that? Do you think that's it?"

"I'm certain it is," Eiler said. He looked up as the guard came in.

"Sorry to disturb you, captain, but Mr. McKitrick wants to send a telegram with your authorization." He handed Eiler a slip of paper and Eiler had difficulty making out the words, so poor was McKitrick's handwriting.

93

Captain:
My wife suggests I need a lawyer. I agree. Will you wire the bank at Ashland, over your signature, and draw out my savings, sixty-eight hundred dollars? If you vouch for the telegram, it will be honored. I've done this before.

McK.

Eiler put the paper on his desk and said, "Mrs. McKitrick, while your husband has been gone on these hunting trips, has he ever wired back to the bank for money?"

"Why, yes," she said, surprised that he would know such a thing. "A year ago he lost his outfit, horse and all, and wired for seven hundred dollars."

"Where did he wire from?"

She wrinkled her brows in thought. "Why, I can't think of the name exactly. I should. He wired once before from there. It's a Mexican name. Someplace near the border."

"Would you recognize it if I said it?"

"Why, I think so."

He started naming them off, starting with Juarez and when he said, "Piedras Negras," she stopped him with a lifted hand.

"Why, I think that's it. I'm sure it is."

He nodded. "Do you think Mr. McKitrick should have a lawyer?"

"I said that to him not twenty minutes ago. I told him when I got home I'd draw the money out of the bank and get a lawyer." She stopped talking and looked at him. "Why did you ask that?"

"Because he wants me to send a telegram to do just that," Eiler said. "Mrs. McKitrick, go back to him. Now you can see that all this is your overworked imagination."

"I'm so grateful to you," she said and he got up and opened the door for her and after she left he sat down at his desk and tapped his pencil without letup for fifteen minutes. Then he went to the door and drew the guard's attention.

"Get Pine. Wake him and get him over here on the double."

Pine came in a few minutes later, picking sleep from his eyes; he was in a sour frame of mind. "Knew I shouldn't have stretched out," he said. "Just knew it." He pointed his finger at Nathan Eiler. "This had better be important. I'm old. I need my sleep."

"Have a drink and you'll feel better," Eiler said. He opened his desk drawer and set out a bottle and Pine took a long pull, then shook his head and shuddered.

"Gawd," he said, "and to think I must have drank twenty gallons of that stuff for fun."

"I had a talk with Mrs. McKitrick," Eiler said. "She strikes me as being a jittery, unhappy woman, who's never felt at ease with her husband."

"So?"

"So we had a talk," Eiler said. "Burke, how well do you know Piedras Negras?"

"Well, I was at Eagle Pass for nearly eight months once."

"Want another drink?" Pine shook his head and Eiler put the bottle away. He sat down and said, "I've drawn some conclusions but I'll need them checked out."

"You want me to go to Piedras Negras?"

"Yes," Eiler said. "McKitrick is known there, or at least he's been there several times because his wife said that he wired back for money. Nothing about this man really turns solid, Burke. Do you know what I mean? If I was checking on you and I learned that you went somewhere, I'd find a reason, like you wanted to get drunk, or wanted a change of scenery, or some foolish, human reason. McKitrick does things for no reason. He carried an outlandish rifle for no real reason; I don't believe the one he gave. He went to Mexico to hunt but there are only wild pigs in that area. He takes a trip each year, but where does he really go? And he never brings anything back with him. Top it all off with the fact that he's a good man on the trail, yet he's lost three outfits, two that he had to replace with money he'd wired home for, and the one he claims he lost crossing the desert."

"He never had an outfit then," Pine said flatly.

"I know that, but I want you to nose around that border country and see what you can pick up. Keep me informed by telegram?"

"Don't I always?" He got up. "When do you want me to start?"

Nathan Eiler seemed surprised. "Why, I was going to light a cigar and before I had it half smoked, I thought I'd hear you riding out."

"Just as I thought; you ain't in no hurry." He grinned and got up and went out and Eiler got out his razor and soap and propped up a mirror on his desk and commenced his morning shave.

Jim Cannon's traveling companion was not Nathan Eiler's idea of an impressive witness. As soon as Cannon came on the post, he went to Eiler's office to wait, for Eiler was out and had to be notified. When he came in, he glanced at the man Cannon had brought along, then said, "Who the devil is this?"

"Jack Gibbon's the handle," the man said, rising unsteadily. "Folks call me Knapsack, mostly. Been livin' out of one for years." He showed Eiler a toothless grin. "Say, you wouldn't have a drink, would you? Been a long, dry ride on the train."

Eiler produced the bottle and a glass and Knapsack Jack poured it half full. He drank most of it without pause, then sighed and leaned back in the chair, his frail legs crossed. "Well, now that does set a man up," he said. "I don't often get a taste of the good stuff."

"Corporal, where did you find this man?" Eiler asked.

"He was recommended to me by the sheriff," Cannon said. "Knapsack is what you'd call a long-time resident. He knows everybody and their business."

"It's a fact," Knapsack said. "Nobody ever bothers a harmless man. You want to hear about me?"

"Unless you came all this way just to drink my whiskey," Eiler said, amused.

"I followed a trail herd north," Knapsack said. "Hides was my business. Always has been and always will be. When a critter died, I'd take the hide. Some people call me a range scavenger, but it's a livin' and nobody's shot at me, which is more than some can say." He finished off his whiskey and put the glass aside. "Knew Kyle Dixon well, and his boy. Knew 'em all well, the ones that got killed and the ones that paid for it, fellas like Price Shatlock and Whitlow and Keene and Maybry . . ."

The steer had died in a bog hole near the spring and he'd had to go back to his camp for a spare rope because he'd snapped one trying to pull the carcass free. It wouldn't do to leave a dead steer in the bog; the spring could be polluted.

This was combine range, owned by Whitlow and Price Shatlock and normally a man riding it uninvited would get shot, but Knapsack Jack was privileged; he could come and go as he pleased and no one bothered him. His old wagon and team was a common sight and no man thought twice about seeing him at any hour or any place, searching the range for dead cattle. He had a cabin but he spent little time there; his wagon and his blankets were his home.

When he got back to the bog hole with the rope he found George Whitlow there and although this surprised Knapsack Jack, it caused him no alarm.

Whitlow said, "Looks like the critter got caught yesterday and plumb wore himself out fightin'."

" 'Pears that way," Knapsack said.

"Saw you heading this way," Whitlow said. "Saw you leave without your wagon so I knew you'd be back." He looked at Knapsack and Knapsack waited; Whitlow wanted something or he wouldn't even be talking to him. "Your teeth been giving you much trouble lately?"

"I've had good days and bad," Knapsack said. "This winter, if I've made enough, I'm goin' to have 'em pulled."

"That'll cost upwards to forty-five dollars," Whitlow said. "Had an uncle who had his out. Know what it costs. A man has enough trouble in this world without having his teeth give him hell." He shifted in the saddle. "I could help you out,

Knapsack. Sort of one good deed deserving another."

"What would I have to do?"

George Whitlow got down and tied his horse. He took a cigar from a case and lit it. "When it comes to pulling teeth, I'd go to Cheyenne. They've got a good dentist there."

"I could do that," Knapsack said, "if I had the train fare."

"That would be taken care of," Whitlow said. He was a stern-faced, blocky man, rather short but heavy through the upper body. He wore jeans and a short jacket, but he sat an expensive saddle and two hundred dollars wouldn't begin to buy his horse. "Knapsack, we've all got our troubles. You've got your teeth vexin' you and I've got— well I've got things that vex me. I want you to meet a man in Cheyenne. You'll make a deal with him. I'll tell you what to say, all you'll need to say." He studied the tip of his cigar a moment. "I trust you, Knapsack. You and me, we can have this little talk here and no one need know anything about it. If it ever got out it would be your word against mine. If anyone sees us talking, why they wouldn't think anything of it because most everyone talks to you. Everyone knows you take no sides between the big cattlemen and these small rawhiders who rustle us blind."

"I guess that's so," Knapsack said.

"So you can go to Cheyenne and get your teeth

pulled and nobody'll think anything of it. Do you see?"

"Yep."

"Good," Whitlow said. "Now I'm going to hire this fella, the one you're going to see. I'll give you an envelope to hand to him. He'll give you one to bring back to me. That's all there is to it."

"I can do that," Knapsack said. "How do I locate this fella anyway?"

"We'll take care of that in time," Whitlow said. "You might tell it around that you're going to Cheyenne to see the dentist."

"When?"

"Within two weeks."

"People know I ain't got any money," Knapsack said. "The hide buyer might add two and two and wonder and mention it around."

"A week from tomorrow," Whitlow said, "come to my place. We're slaughtering eight head. You can have the hides. That'll be your stake." He smiled. "And in case it ever comes up, I didn't give you a dime." A sound from the other side of the spring drew his attention, then a buggy appeared over the brow of a small rise and came on down the trail to the spring.

A man and boy sat side by side on the seat and the man hauled up. "Howdy, Whitlow."

"What are you doing here, Dixon?"

"It's my spring." He pointed to the dead steer. "Looks like one of mine." He reached into his pocket for cut plug and bit off a chew. Then he handed the reins to his son and got down, crossed over and looked at the animal from the other side. "Can you get it out, Knapsack?"

"Never had one yet I couldn't."

Whitlow said, "Dixon, I warned you to stay away from this spring."

"That's right, you did," Dixon said. He was a tall, well-made man with a dark complexion and a blunt, fearless manner. He was a Texan, but unlike Whitlow, he was a poor Texan trying to make a go of it in a new country, and he was having a hard time of it. Pneumonia the first winter had taken his wife, and the big cattlemen, represented by Price Shatlock, with Whitlow as spokesman, worked hard to squeeze him off his section.

Whitlow said, "The trouble with you, Dixon, is that you don't hear too good."

"I hear what I need to hear," Dixon said. "The rest is just so much wind blowing. When my wire comes, I'm going to fence this spring."

"I told you not to do that," George Whitlow said.

Dixon smiled. "The wind's blowin' again," he said and went to his buggy and got aboard. Then he drove back over the rise and disappeared.

Whitlow said, "We've got a deal, Knapsack." He mounted up and rode out and Jack Gibbon got out his block and tackle and went to work getting the dead steer out of the bog.

• • •

He didn't often go near Price Shatlock's headquarters; he had no business there and the long-reaching Shatlock power rather held him away. Not many men knew where Price Shatlock was or would be at any given time, for he was always on the go. He had vast ranch property in Texas and a private railway coach to carry him around and he came and went with a flurry. When he came to town, there'd be a flurry of trouble for someone and good news for Price Shatlock, and not many people drew a decent breath when he was around.

Knapsack timed his arrival for dusk. He rode to the horse corrals and stayed there until someone saw him and told Whitlow, who came out and took him to the house. Not inside, but to the porch where Price Shatlock sat, all six foot three of him with his white suit and pearl-handled pistol and hundred-dollar boots.

Shatlock studied Knapsack Jack for a moment, then said, "He don't look like much, Whitlow." Shatlock was in his mid-forties, a bony-faced man who liked scowling better than smiling. "You stink, man. Don't you ever take a bath and clean up?"

"Well, if I got a river to cross and the weather's warm, I've got nothing against it," Knapsack said, smiling.

Whitlow spoke sternly. "Keep your mouth shut. Mr. Shatlock didn't expect an answer."

"Then how come he asked me?" Knapsack said.

"This man's a fool," Price Shatlock said.

"I guess I am," Knapsack said, "but I ain't bein' shot at by your riders and I ain't hated by the nesters."

Shatlock stared at him for a moment, then laughed heartily. "You've got nerve. I like it. Whitlow will give you the hides. Sell them in the morning, then get a bath and a shave and a suit of clothes and your ticket to Cheyenne. Make a fuss about it. I want everyone in town to know you're going to get your teeth fixed. And mister, you come back without one in your head, you understand?"

"Don't need to worry about that," Knapsack said.

"I never worry," Shatlock said. "I plan well, then I don't have to worry. Whitlow will give you an envelope. You take it with you. In Cheyenne, go to the Drover's Hotel; anyone there can tell you where it is. There'll be a number on the outside of the envelope. That's a room number. Go there at ten o'clock at night. You scratch on the door like a dog wanting in; don't knock. A man will let you in. Give him the envelope. He'll ask you some questions. You answer him."

Knapsack Jack scratched his head. "Will I know the answers?"

"You'll know the answers," Whitlow said.

"It sounds simple enough," Knapsack said. "Is that all?"

"The man will give you an envelope to take back to me," Shatlock said. "See that I get it."

"All right," Knapsack said. "Do I know this fella?"

"You've never seen him and you never will," Shatlock said. "I've never seen him either, and if you did get a look at him, your life wouldn't be worth the price of a rotten hide." He waved his hand. "Get him his hides, Whitlow, and get him out of here."

"Come on," Whitlow said and Knapsack followed him to the barn. The hides were by the west side and Knapsack loaded them and when he was finished he took a bottle from under the seat and drank from it.

"My teeth have been givin' me hell today," he said and took another drink before putting the bottle away. He looked toward the house and said, "It kind of gives a man the quivers, this business."

"Do it right and you have nothing to worry about," Whitlow advised.

"I've seen some gunfighters," Knapsack said, "but a professional killer I ain't never seen."

"They're the kind you don't see," Whitlow said. "And when it comes right down to it, a man's not liable to want to."

Knapsack climbed aboard his wagon and lifted the reins, then said, "I got a funny way to make a livin'; most folks wouldn't think of it or want it. I guess this fella's got a funny way too. How does a man like that get started without showin' himself?"

Whitlow remained silent for a moment, then said, "There was some trouble five years ago, right after Mr. Shatlock took over here. You might remember it. One day he got a package in the mail. It was a .45-70 bullet with a man's name carved in the lead. That man's name was someone Mr. Shatlock could well do without."

"Cliff Orland," Knapsack said. "By God!"

"It wouldn't pay you to mention that," Whitlow said. "We're just talking, Knapsack, the way men do. There was a note wrapped around the bullet, with the name of a town, a hotel, a room number, and a date and a time to be there. There was also a price. High, but a man gets what he pays for." He reached up and put his hand on Knapsack's leg and squeezed. "A man knows what he knows and keeps it under his hat. You're like that, Knapsack. If you weren't, I'll bet you wouldn't live another thirty days." Then he stepped back. "I hope the dentist does a good job on your teeth."

"Like you say, a man gets what he pays for," Knapsack said and drove out of the yard.

Chapter Seven

The hide buyer paid top rate for the hides and Knapsack Jack Gibbon folded this wealth, then sauntered on down the street to the barbershop. He paid thirty-five cents for the bath, twenty-five cents for the haircut, and fifteen cents for his shave, and the transformation was so great that the clerk in the general store failed to identify him right off.

A change of clothes and a train ticket later, Knapsack sat on one of the depot benches and counted the remainder of his money, more than enough to have his teeth pulled. Inside his coat, in an inner pocket, was the envelope that Whitlow had given him; he would move his arm now and then to make the paper rustle, assuring himself that it was still there, and safe.

He supposed that by nightfall everyone in town would know where he was going and why, and that was the way Price Shatlock wanted it. It was the way he wanted it too because he didn't want to be connected with all this trouble. He remembered all too clearly the time Cliff Orland and his wife had been killed. Burke Pine had been the sheriff and if ever Knapsack had seen a man possessed it had been Pine. No one ever gave him one whoop in hell of ever finding the killer, but Pine had surprised them all by bringing in one of

Shatlock's riders. What the rider had told Pine, Knapsack Jack never knew, but a week later the rider had taken a tumble from his horse and had been dragged to death.

It was exactly the kind of sad accident a man could expect to have when he made Price Shatlock unhappy.

Knapsack got aboard his train, found a seat in the day coach, and went to sleep. Noisy children and chatting women and a rough roadbed failed to wake him; the conductor did it just as they pulled into the station, and Knapsack got off and looked around. Cheyenne was a bigger town than he had expected and walking along the main street, Knapsack Jack found himself lost in the crowd. There was a good deal of mounted and wagon traffic and he had to wait several minutes before he could cross. He found a dentist in an upstairs office, talked over his problem, submitted to an examination, and made his appointment for the next morning. The doctor prided himself on using the most modern methods, and promised that a hypodermic injection would render the whole operation painless, and would bed and board Knapsack for three days following, until stitches could be safely removed.

And all for a fee of forty-seven dollars; Knapsack felt that he had made one of life's truly great bargains.

Loafing in a strange town irritated him; he had to know people to enjoy himself. His drinking was even limited because he needed a clear head later on in the night, so he nursed a glass of beer and played solitaire until it was dark.

He hated to spend the fifty cents, but he ate in a restaurant, passing up the coffee and apple pie because it would set up an agony in his teeth. Two walks up and down each side of the street and it was time; he went into the hotel, circulated briefly, and when he was sure that he attracted no attention he went up the stairs and down a long hall.

Number twenty-six was on his right and he raised his hand to knock, then remembered and scratched instead. There was a strong light coming from under the door and a voice said, "Come in."

Knapsack stepped inside and blinked, for two lamps, backed by mirrors, hit him in the eyes. The man said, "Lock the door, and then sit in that chair."

The chair was in the middle of the room and Knapsack sat down in it.

"Do you have something for me?"

Taking the envelope out of his pocket, Knapsack handed it over and the man opened it. He counted the money, well over a thousand dollars. There was a picture too but Knapsack couldn't see who it was. But he could see the man's hands, round and stubby-fingered. Then the man drew them back behind the light.

Knapsack said, "I can't see nothin' with them lamps shinin' in my eyes."

"There's nothing for you to see," the man said. "How well do you know the country where you live?"

"As good as any man," Knapsack said.

"Is Burke Pine still sheriff?"

Knapsack shook his head. "He left six months after Orland and his wife was murdered. The last I heard, he's in the Texas Rangers."

"Who's the law?"

"A Shatlock man," Knapsack said.

"Whose man are you?"

"My own," Knapsack said. "I'm here because I want to be. If I didn't want to be, I wouldn't be. And if I wanted a look at you bad enough, I'd take it."

"You'd die for it."

"If I wanted to bad enough, then I'd be willing to do that too," he said. "Anything else you want to know?"

"Nothing I can't find out for myself," the man said. He handed Knapsack an envelope. "You can go. I've found out all I want to know."

Knapsack got up and unlocked the door; he hesitated a second then stepped out into the hall and went down to the lobby. He hung around the clerk's desk until the man grew busy, then he swiveled the register around and found number twenty-six: Calvin Reed.

He managed to put the register back as the clerk turned; he said, "Did you want a room, sir?"

"Thanks, no," Knapsack said and walked out.

He paused on the porch just out of the main stream of traffic and wondered how he'd locate Calvin Reed among all these people, then the answer came to him, so simple that he cursed himself for not thinking of it before. He turned and went back inside the hotel and stepped up to the clerk's desk.

"Danged near forgot what I meant to ask you," Knapsack said. "I'm looking for a friend of mine, Calvin Reed. Is he stayin' here?"

"Room twenty-six," the clerk said. "But he's at the Bird Cage playing poker. I saw him go in there an hour ago when I stepped out for a sandwich." A man approached the desk and the clerk left Knapsack and a moment later he was busy assigning a room; Knapsack left the hotel and went over to the saloon to get a drink of whiskey; his teeth were bothering him again.

"I should have knowed," Knapsack said, puffing on one of Eiler's cigars, "that Tass Creel was too smart to be caught that way."

"You never got a look at anything but his hands?" Eiler asked.

"That's all. Of course I could see a shadow of a

man behind the lamps, but that was all," Knapsack said.

Nathan Eiler said, "You've held this information for years. Tell me why you've come forward with it now?"

"Shatlock is dead," Knapsack said. "And Cannon here tells me he thinks he's got Tass Creel behind bars."

"I see," Eiler said, frowning. "The part you played in this led to a man's murder. You can be tried for that, you know."

"Could be, but I'm bettin' you won't go to the trouble," Knapsack said. "You ain't never goin' to get Whitlow to admit nothin'. There was six men in the cattle combine, but two got themselves killed. Whitlow, Keene, and Maybry remained. And Shatlock." He shook his head. "You wouldn't have a case againse me, captain. And you know it."

Eiler sighed and gnawed on his dead cigar. His glance touched Jim Cannon. "You said you had proof that the boy, Charlie Dixon, was alive."

"He's alive," Knapsack said flatly. "That's the rest of the story."

With gums still too tender to eat solid food, Knapsack lived on soup and coffee and pan biscuits. He'd been back on the range for a week, back to his old business of moving around, watching the herds.

As soon as he got back, Whitlow had looked him up and taken the envelope and ridden out without a word; he was through with Knapsack and felt no need for talk.

A rider found him in the early afternoon and told him there was a dead steer across the swale near Kyle Dixon's place, and Knapsack hitched up his wagon and drove over there, arriving just before sunset. He had time, he figured, to set up camp and skin out. He could leave in the morning. There was a creek nearby and firewood and one place was pretty much like the other.

He was camped on the side of a hill and he could see Dixon's place in the distance, and a portion of the road leading on into town, and before dark he saw Dixon leave his yard with his boy beside him on the buggy.

Knapsack thought nothing of it for he saw a lot of people moving around, but now and then he glanced toward the road to measure Dixon's progress. The road took a sharp cut following the flat valley, and disappeared between two rises, and he saw Dixon turn and afterward—he figured later maybe five minutes—he heard the boom of a heavy caliber rifle. Catching up one of his horses, he started out bareback, cutting down off the hill to meet the road farther down.

He found the buggy, and Kyle Dixon, the right side of his head blown away, but there was no sign of the boy, or of the man who had fired the shot. Darkness was coming on fast, and Knapsack rode around the rig until he picked up a scar in the grass made by a small boot moving in a hurry.

Getting down off his horse, he led the animal and started out, working up the flank of the hill, but working carefully, sniffing as he went, crouched over, picking up the faint aroma of crushed grass.

The trail petered out on him when the ground turned rocky, but he could smell freshly-stirred dust and knew that he was going in the right direction. From above there came the rattle of loose stones rolling, and he moved faster, climbing nearly to the summit of the hill. And he found the boy there with his father's gun and he would have shot Knapsack if he hadn't grabbed it and torn it from his hand.

The boy began to fight and he was a strong fifteen; Knapsack had to hit him to quiet him. Then he said, "Charlie, Charlie, it's me, Knapsack."

Young Dixon began to cry and Knapsack slapped him and there was no more crying. From below, a horse made stones roll and it was all the warning Knapsack needed.

"We've got to get out of here," he said and led the boy down the other side of the slope. Only he didn't go far, but cut along the hill's flank until he found a good hiding place and they waited there while the shadowy horseman carefully eased on past and down the slope. Then Knapsack moved out with the boy and returned to his horse on the road. He mounted, hoisted the boy behind him and they rode away, carefully, making no noise.

All that night, and part of the next morning, they spent moving to the most southern corner of Price Shatlock's range. Charlie Dixon was calmer now; he knew he could not go back to the home place or even attend his father's funeral.

"We've got to get you out of the country, Charlie," Knapsack said. "I don't expect you got any money." The boy shook his head. "Well, I've got fourteen dollars. You got any place to go? Any kin?"

"Pa's sister in Texas," Charlie Dixon said.

"We'll get you there somehow," Knapsack said. "It's a terrible thing, these goin's on. Terrible to lose your pa and be turned out with only the clothes on your back. In the mornin' we'll start south until we reach the railroad. There's a telegraph station there where you can get aboard the train."

"Someday," Charlie Dixon said faintly, "I'm going to get Price Shatlock. Just the way he got Pa."

"Now you don't want to talk like that," Knapsack said. "Ain't there been enough killin'?"

"Everyone thinks Shatlock is too big to be stopped. I know he ain't. I'll get him. You wait and see." He looked at Knapsack Jack Gibbon. "I know you don't have much and I guess you've offered it all to me, and I won't forget that either."

"Shucks, you didn't think I'd stand by and let that killer get you, did you?"

"You think I'm a kid, makin' big talk. I'm not. You wait and see."

It was all he had to say; that day and the next he remained stone silent and then they reached the telegraph station. Knapsack bought his ticket and gave him the three dollars and eight cents change.

He waited that night and the next morning and saw Charlie Dixon on the southbound, then he turned back north to tend to his own business.

"I never saw him again," Knapsack said and got up to walk over to Eiler's east window. "But I'm not likely to forget him, captain. He was a boy when he got in his father's buggy, but he was a man when I put him on that train. He had a man's coldness in the eye, and a man's determination in him. When Cannon told me Shatlock had been killed, and that Creel had done it, I wondered then if Charlie Dixon had kept his promise."

"By God," Nathan Eiler said, "what a possibility. Jim, get Judge Rainsford and Colonel Lavery in here. And you might as well invite Fred Sheridan; he may be able to help us here."

Cannon went out and Knapsack turned to look at Eiler. "Did I say somethin' good for a change?"

116

"You're worth your weight in Kentucky whiskey," Eiler said.

Judge Rainsford was the first to arrive; he was introduced to Knapsack Jack Gibbon, then Paul Lavery came in. All these important people made Knapsack uneasy and he turned his back on them for a moment while he fumbled in his jacket pocket. When he turned back he was wearing a perfect set of "store" teeth. Eiler was bringing Rainsford and the colonel up to date; he was saying, "I want a warrant issued for the arrest of Whitlow, Keene, and Maybry."

"Three pretty important gentlemen," Rainsford pointed out. "Just an academic point. I'll issue the warrants."

"I've got to find the man who paid Creel to do the Shatlock job," Eiler said. He heard a step approach the door and looked around. "Ah, come in, Sheridan. You might be able to help us here." He turned to the other. "I believe you know these gentlemen, with the exception of Mr. Gibbon."

There was a moment when the two men looked at each other, then they shook hands and Knapsack mumbled something only half intelligible.

"As I was saying, Sheridan, we now have strong reason to believe we've found a suspect who triggered Shatlock's death. I could sincerely use your newspaper."

"I'll do what I can, captain," Sheridan said.

"Fine. Now I'd like some editorial pressure brought to bear on Whitlow, Keene, and Maybry. Judge Rainsford is issuing a warrant for their arrest so they can be questioned, but it would be much better if they walked into the nearest ranger station and offered themselves up."

"I've been writing about them off and on for some years," Sheridan said. "A little more won't hurt."

"This whole thing is beginning to come together a little now," Eiler said. "Shatlock was killed out of revenge, and the man who hired Creel to do the job has got to be found."

"Revenge?" Sheridan asked. "Revenge for what, captain?"

"Kyle Dixon's death," Eiler said. "It looks now like Charlie Dixon, the man, paid Creel to do the job."

For a moment, Sheridan remained silent, then he said, "That ought to make a real story. Have you located Dixon?"

"No," Eiler said. "But we will. One of those three, Whitlow, Maybry, or Keene, may be able to lead us to Dixon. Someone, somewhere, knows how to contact Creel. Dixon found out for he hired the very man who murdered his father. If you want to know what I think, I believe it was this fear of dying that led Price Shatlock to offer himself up and testify. He'd rather spend the rest of his life in prison and take his friends with him than be killed. Unfortunately, it didn't work that way."

"Surely Whitlow or one of the others could have contacted Creel," Sheridan said.

"Of course that's possible," Eiler said. "We know Whitlow contacted Creel once, or had it done through Knapsack."

Sheridan slowly turned his head and looked at the old man. Then he said, "When was this?"

"Before the Kyle Dixon killing," Eiler said, then turned to Rainsford. "I don't want to seem in a hurry, judge, but—"

"Of course, I'll get on it right away," Rainsford said. "Care to join me, Colonel Lavery? We'll have dinner together later."

"I will if there's no more need of me here," Lavery said.

There wasn't and he went out with Rainsford. Knapsack was standing with his back to them, looking out the window; his manner thoughtfully grave.

Jim Cannon said, "Captain, with your permission, I'll go in town."

"Of course," Eiler said. "Take tomorrow off. You might show Mr. Gibbon some quarters."

"Why, I'll do that," Fred Sheridan said. "The corporal's probably in a hurry to go home and see his family and I've got a lot of time on my hands."

"Thank you," Eiler said and cleared the office.

Cannon mounted up and rode on into town and

Sheridan and Knapsack Jack walked toward the barrack tents. Neither man spoke for a time, then Sheridan said, "A lot of strange facts come to light in this kind of an investigation, don't they? Now to look at you, a man would think you were a nice old guy that never hurt anyone. But that's not so, is it?"

Knapsack stopped and looked at Sheridan. "Get to the point."

"Why, I've got none, really. Do you think they'll ever find Charlie Dixon?"

"How would I know?" Knapsack asked. He squinted at Fred Sheridan. "Charlie Dixon would be dead if it wasn't for me."

"And his father would have been alive if it wasn't for you," Sheridan said.

"Friend, no power on earth would have stopped Shatlock from havin' him killed. I did it because it was goin' to be done, and I wouldn't have lasted long if I'd turned Whitlow down. Yeah, he come to me with the deal, but it was Shatlock who gave the orders. I was there."

"Then there was no mistake," Sheridan said. "Shatlock got what he had coming."

"Not the way he got it," Knapsack said. "No man deserves it that way." He turned to walk on, but Sheridan took his arm and held him.

"You seem to be a man who can keep his mouth shut, Knapsack."

"That I am. I don't give nothin' away."

"Why did you come here with the ranger then?"

"To see Tass Creel caught," Knapsack said. "Know a better reason?" He gave his arm a jerk and freed himself from Sheridan's grip. "You write for a newspaper. All right, then write a message for Charlie Dixon. Tell him he's as bad as Shatlock no matter what reasons he has. Tell him to make tracks, to lose himself before it's too late."

"Maybe he's gone too far now to stop."

"A man never gets that far. Not even Shatlock," Knapsack said and walked on to the barracks tent.

A ranger fixed him up with an empty bunk and the old man stretched out and looked at the ridge pole. A sense of uneasiness filled him now and he wished he were back on his place in Wyoming. It wasn't much, just a hundred and sixty acres, but he had water and some good pasture and ran a few head of beef and kept a nice garden and it was enough to satisfy him.

Wyoming had changed. The big Texas men weren't so big now and the little man didn't have to worry about someone throwing a torch in his haystack or shooting him from the saddle on some lonely road.

And all this came about in the most unexpected way. The Texas money and the big ranches got just so big and then there wasn't anything else to take from the little fellow and they began to look at each other like fat hogs eyeing another bushel

121

of corn. Then they began eating and there was no stopping it; they killed each other off and rode each other out and formed cattlemen's protective associations to disguise bands of outlaws and when the shooting died off and the land was all broken up again, all a man had to do was to go in there and drive his stakes.

He'd built a very solid cabin on the foundations of one burned to the ground, and in a few years he bought the land for back taxes, proving what he had always believed, that any man could have what he wanted if he could only wait long enough.

He ate in the mess tent and the food was good and afterward he stopped at the watering trough to rinse off his teeth. Then he decided he'd walk on into town and maybe buy a beer and look at the sights. When he went back he wanted something to talk about, and there wasn't anything going on at the ranger post; the place was like an army post with a lot of men running around when the sergeant yelled.

He found Rock Springs a lively little town. The odor of beer and the sound of tinny piano music drew him to the saloon and he bellied up to the bar and presented his money; he had learned a long time ago that he couldn't get a drink on appearances' sake.

A shot of whiskey chased by warm beer started a mild fire in his stomach and he listened to the piano for awhile, then went out and walked up and down the street. He spent some time peering into the store windows and even went into the general store and cruised around the displayed merchandise for he liked the smell of fresh coffee and good leather and at the cheese case he paused for his slice, dipping into the cracker barrel on the way out.

The traffic drew his interest and he walked up and down both sides of the main street, looking carefully at the horses and saddles; he admired animals and the Mexican saddles interested him, for a few were loaded with nickel-plated trappings. A man's gear, he knew, reflected a lot about the owner and the work he did and the part of the country he was from. In brush country you'd never see a man with his rifle scabbarded butt forward, or wearing a saddle with a lot of trappings; those things were a nuisance.

He wore out the display of saddle horses, and at the dark end of the street he paused, wondering what to do next. A slight sound near a gap between two buildings caused him to turn his head, then a man said, "Pssssttt, come here."

Curiosity made him step that way and he was almost even with the gap when he stopped and started to recoil. But it was too late for the man grabbed him with his left hand, pulled him into the gap and mashed him against the side of the building.

The knife went in quick and deep and he gasped and then his legs gave way and the man let him fall. He stood there in the complete darkness, looking at Knapsack on the ground, both hands clasped to his stomach.

"I—I wouldn't—have said—"

The rest was a bubbly sigh and he fell back, his head cocked over to one side, his hands falling away from his fatal wound. The man stood there a moment, then turned and quickly, noiselessly made his way to the alley and disappeared.

Chapter Eight

George Whitlow surrendered himself to a ranger detachment near his ranch in north Texas and almost immediately, in the company of a ranger, he boarded the southbound train for Rock Springs.

He arrived in the morning in time for Knapsack Jack Gibbon's funeral and Eiler saw that he attended. Whitlow was an old man, his hair white now, and deep wrinkles creased his face, and when he looked at Knapsack tucked into the satin-pillowed casket he seemed much older, as though the sight of the man made him realize just how much time had gone by.

After the funeral they went back to Eiler's office; Sheriff Owen Henry was waiting on the porch and Henry had his jaw tight and trouble in his eye.

He started off by saying, "I don't see why the goddamn hell this nonsense isn't over. You've held McKitrick long enough and proved nothing." He jabbed Eiler in the chest with his finger. "Now I want to know when you're releasing him."

"When I do, I'll tell you," Eiler said and brushed past him. Jim Cannon followed, urging George Whitlow ahead of him; he closed the office door and motioned Whitlow into a chair.

"Poor old Knapsack," Whitlow said. "The old bastard never got much out of life."

"A set of teeth," Eiler said. "But he paid a hell of a price for them." He pointed his finger at Whitlow. "Now we might as well get something straight. There's nothing about your fortune or your prominence in the State of Texas that impresses me two whoops in hell. You're implicated in crime that stretches over an eighteen year period and implicated right up to your eyeballs. Now it may be that you have enough money to buy the best lawyers in the world. It may be that you can find a judge you can buy, and a jury, but one thing for sure, you can bet your hat and ass that you're going to be prosecuted." He lowered his voice. "Now I don't need your testimony to put you in jail, Mr. Whitlow. I have Jack Gibbon's testimony before witnesses. And I'm not making any deals with you, promising you a slap on the wrist if you volunteer any statements. You'll get just what Price Shatlock accepted, a chance to make a clean sweep of it, and a chance to throw yourself on the mercy of the court. Some of you Texas men have burned and bullied and killed for a few more sections of land, for a few more thousand dollars, when you had so much you couldn't possibly spend it. Be sure you understand the terms, Mr. Whitlow."

George Whitlow sat for a time, just looking at Nathan Eiler. Then he said, "A friend of mine in Austin said there wasn't an inch of give in you, and damned little mercy." He sighed and studied his wrinkled, pink hands. There was no sign of callus or scar, no indication that they had ever turned out a day's work. "I'm seventy-one, captain. Most of that time I've lived in fear of someone, or of something. Price Shatlock owned my soul for right onto twenty-one years. I didn't cry a damned bit when Creel put a bullet in him."

"Shatlock never got a chance to talk," Eiler pointed out. "Didn't it worry you, what he would say?"

"No," Whitlow said. "I could always deny it. Maybe I wouldn't get away with all of it, but I was willing to gamble I wouldn't hang for it either." He leaned back in his chair, one arm thrown over the back. "I got the message one day at my ranch that Shatlock had to see me; he made it sound important enough, so I took the train that night to San Angelo . . ."

The weather was turning chilly and Whitlow was happy to see that Shatlock had a rig waiting for him. A crusty driver sat on the seat while Whitlow wrestled with his suitcase, then Whitlow got in and before he settled on the seat, the driver whipped the team into motion and took the south road out of town.

Shatlock's place was a mansion set in a grove of trees, and the lights downstairs were bright in every room when they pulled along the curved drive and stopped. A negro servant ran out and took Whitlow's bag and ushered him to the door where another negro in butler's livery conducted him down the long hall to a library.

Keene and Maybry were already there and although these men had not been together for three years, they merely nodded, as though they were total strangers.

Price Shatlock sat near the fireplace, a thin man with worry in his eyes. He said, "You took your time, Whitlow."

"I'm not your dog to jump anymore," Whitlow said. "What do you want, Price?"

"I called you here together because I want an answer," Shatlock said. He reached into his coat pocket and took out a .45-70 bullet and placed it on its base on a table. "Bend closer and look at the carving in the lead. That's my name, Price Shatlock. Which one of you paid Creel to send it to me?"

A slackness came into their faces and they looked at each other and at Shatlock. Whitlow spoke. "I sure as hell didn't. But I'm not saying that it isn't a good idea." He sat down. "You look pretty scared, Price. They say that Tass Creel never misses."

"Very funny," Shatlock said. He looked at Keene and Maybry. "I suppose you don't know anything about this either?" They shook their heads, and he laughed without humor. "That's just

128

what I expected. All right, I'll tell you what I'm going to do. I'm going someplace where even Tass Creel can't reach me. This morning, I sent a telegram to Captain Nathan Eiler, Company B, Texas Rangers. Right now there's two of his best men on the way here to take me to Rock Springs. I'm going to do some talking, boys. How do you like them apples?"

"You wouldn't put a rope around your neck," Keene said. He was a small, prune-faced man with dark piercing eyes.

"I don't intend to hang," Shatlock said. "But I might have to spend a few years as a guest of the state. I'm going to make it hard for Creel to earn his three thousand this time."

"For you he ought to get more," Maybry said.

Shatlock glared at him. "How much did you have to pay?"

Maybry laughed. "Go to hell, Price. You get nothing out of me."

"It seems to me," Keene said, "that you've jumped to some wrong conclusions, Price. Or you've forgotten that someone else could have hired Tass Creel."

"Like whom?" Shatlock asked.

Keene shrugged. "You left a lot of blood spilled in Wyoming. Someone there—"

"Hell, the ones with guts are gone," he snapped. "They were ready to forget. I know their kind. One tough punch and the fight's gone."

"You can't talk to him," Whitlow said. "What's the use of trying?"

"That's right," Maybry said. "You haven't changed, Price. You get your mind on something and there's no prying you loose." He opened his cigar case and passed it around. "Is that all you got, the bullet?"

"There was a note wrapped around it." He took it from his pocket and handed it to Maybry. "It doesn't make sense to me."

Maybry moved around so the light was at his back.

Shatlock:
For five hundred more you could have killed the boy.

Mabry handed the note to Whitlow, who read it and said, "Why you damned fool, don't you remember? Dixon had a son! He disappeared."

For a moment Price Shatlock sat there, then he nodded. "Of course, I remember now. Dixon did have a boy. No one ever saw him again." He sighed heavily. "If those rangers don't get here, I'm a dead man."

"Now you know who paid Creel," Keene said. "I ought to make you apologize."

"Leave him alone," Whitlow said. "Price, how do you suppose he got a message through to Creel?"

"Through the paper, of course," Shatlock said. "Or someone recommended him, told him what to put in the paper. Creel worked for others too, you know." Then Shatlock laughed. "I'd like to have been there when he told Creel who he wanted killed. Young Dixon probably doesn't figure it to this day, the bargain he got."

"What do you mean?" Keene asked.

Shatlock looked at him wryly. "Why, Tass Creel wouldn't charge him a dime for this job. I know him too well. And he told me once that all he'd killed were little men. Someday he was going to shoot someone big, like me." He leaned back in his chair and put his cigar in the ashtray. "I wonder how many thousands of men have seen Tass Creel, men he associates with every day, and none of them suspect who he is. As far as I know, I'm the only man alive who's seen him and known who he was. That's bothered him from time to time, I know, because he's not sure I know him on sight. He suspects and that's all. I did it very cleverly."

"I didn't know any of this," Keene said. "But I guess there's a lot about you that I don't know."

"Hell, who really knows anyone?" Shatlock said. "I raised my family with love, and I helped build my state and I've been bad and good and who the hell can say where one begins and the other ends. I gave up trying a long time ago." He picked up his cigar, punched ash from the dead end and relit it. "A long time ago I got another bullet in the mail, and a note telling me how to contact Tass Creel if I was interested." He chuckled. "I went through the hokus-pokus with the lights shining in my face and I paid the money and he did the job. Then I got another note telling me that if I ever needed him again, or wanted to recommend him, to put an ad in the Eagle Pass paper, and it was to read: *Need you at home, son.* It was to be signed: *Uncle Charlie,* with all replies to be addressed to the newspaper. Of course, they had my address and would send any message on."

"He knew how to cover his tracks," Whitlow said.

"He did at that," Shatlock said. "But I'm not a stupid man and I like to know who I'm doing business with." He smiled slyly. "So I made a trip to Eagle Pass and I talked to the newspaper man there. He told me that 'son' hadn't replied locally, but had mailed a letter. The trouble was, he'd taken the message out, relayed it to me, and thrown the envelope away. There wasn't anything I could do then, but I sold him a good story. I told him the boy was a little wild and that he was in my care since his folks had died and that we worried some about his whereabouts. A twenty-dollar gold piece set the deal, and the next message he got, he mailed the envelope along with it. Then I knew where Creel was from, and I wrote the newspaperman and asked him who in that Kansas town read his paper. Came right back with a name, so I took the next train north for a look at Creel face to face. You see, I'd caught a look at his hands from behind the light, kind of chubby with short fingers. And now that I knew his name, and saw him, I knew I'd made my man."

"For God's sake," Keene said, "who is he?"

"Owen Henry, the damned sheriff," Shatlock said. "Henry subscribed to the Eagle Pass paper, and had been a subscriber for years. He was a short, round-bellied man with fat hands and chubby fingers, and he had the kind of a face anyone would trust with his horse, woman, or money." Shatlock shrugged. "He pretended not to know me. Never let on a sign and I was in town for three days. Yes, he's about the smartest, sneakiest man I ever saw. We played poker in the evenings and I even met some of his friends, and I waited, thinking he'd drop some sign, but he never did. So I figured that if he wanted to play the game that way, it was all right with me."

"You could have got yourself killed," Whitlow said. "Creel, or Henry, is a dangerous man with no conscience at all."

"I wasn't afraid of Creel in a stand-up fight," Shatlock said, "and I wasn't about to turn my back on him. But knowing who he was changed nothing; we went through the same rigmarole every time I had a job for him. It never changed.

Nothing did, the way he worked, or the results he always got."

Maybry said, "Price, I'd wire this whole story to the Texas Rangers."

"Already thought of it, but it wouldn't work," Shatlock said. "How could I prove it? A man that careful, that clever, would have covered his tracks too well." He shook his head. "Oh, I'll tell the rangers all right, but I don't expect them to do anything about it."

"How much are you going to tell about us?" Whitlow asked.

"Enough to hurt a little," Shatlock said. "But for old times' sake, I want you to do something for me, no matter what happens. I want you to find Charlie Dixon. I want it to be Creel's last job, because I want you to have the law spring a trap on him. He may get me because I'm not fool enough to think I'm the one to spoil his record. But I want the Dixon kid killed. Hate to do that because I'm too old to care about revenge. But Creel's got to have a target and it couldn't be just anyone; he'd suspect something. Dixon he knows and he'd take the job."

Maybry said, "Price, you're bound for hell for sure."

"I'll have company when you get there," he said. Then he laughed. "Why the long faces? Good Lord, you had your time, didn't you? You made your fortunes and had people jump when you spoke. What do you want? Everything for free?"

"We're all getting on in years," Keene said. "Price, we've got families and respectability. A man doesn't want to throw that away."

"The trouble with you boys," Price Shatlock said, "is that you don't know how to lose."

Nathan Filer had three trays brought to his office, for himself, Jim Cannon, and George Whitlow. For a time he did not speak, then he said, "Your wife will hate me, Jim, but—"

"I know, sir," Cannon said, rising. "The night train?"

"Yes, don't waste any time." He looked at his watch. "You have a little better than an hour. Go on home and I'll send someone in with the search warrants. We've pretty well established Creel's comings and goings. Check on Henry. The man can't be in two places at the same time."

"Don't you believe Shatlock?" Whitlow asked.

"I believe what checks out to be facts," Eiler said. "If Owen Henry was out of town at the time Shatlock was killed here, then we can proceed further." He looked at George Whitlow. "In the meantime, you can be our guest; we have some vacant cells. And if Owen Henry is Tass Creel we won't have much of a problem there because Henry's here on the post."

He let Whitlow stare and finished his meal.

Cannon went out, got his horse from the stable and rode back to town and his home. His wife was fixing the evening meal and he peeled some potatoes for her and told her that he'd have to be gone three or four days.

Before he had finished eating, a ranger came with two search warrants, and a little later Cannon packed a small valise, and walked to the gate with his wife. After he kissed her, he said, "Aren't you putting on a little weight, Jane?"

"Well, I did before," she said.

"Before what?" Then his eyes got round. "Another?"

She smiled. "Well, he's outgrowing his baby clothes and you know how you are about waste and—" He put his hand gently over her mouth.

"I'm going to have to make sergeant to support an increase in the family," he said.

"You will," she said. "Jim, how is it going?"

He frowned thoughtfully. "To tell you the truth, Jane, I don't know. But a lot of things have changed. Pine and I have hunted down quite a few men and we'd bring 'em in with handcuffs on and they'd get tried for rustlin' or murder or somethin' and I never thought much about those things. I don't really think I ever knew what murder was before, or what any man was like who killed another. I'm learnin', Jane. It'll make me better."

He kissed her again and got on his horse and rode to the depot. A flunky there took the animal to the stable where someone from the ranger camp would pick him up. Cannon bought his ticket and got aboard the train and when the daylight played out, he pulled his hat over his eyes and tried to sleep.

The fact that he was going to be a father again pleased him for he was a family man in spite of the time he had to spend away from home. No matter where he was, he thought only of the time when he'd be home, and he counted those brief times carefully for they were of great value to him.

One of these days he'd be promoted to sergeant, and if he kept his record clean, he might even make lieutenant and get an office job where he could spend more time at home. It wasn't, to his way of thinking, a matter of putting home before everything else; he didn't do that. But he wanted to live a normal life, not years of lonely existence with only a good saddle and a pearl-handled six-shooter to his name when he died. A man needed to have a family, to give something of himself to a woman and children so he'd go on even after he was gone.

His thoughts revolved around to Tass Creel; a more twisted man he had never met. But then, he'd never studied any of the men he had apprehended, and he supposed that was a weakness. A good peace officer had to know criminals, had to understand them; it was a part of his education that had up to now been neglected.

Creel was two men and no man at all and maybe a little of all men and Jim Cannon wondered what it was like to live like that, two complete lives, one poles apart from the other. And he wondered what Creel thought of when he stalked his man. Maybe he was looking for another long shot, one of the greatest he had ever made in his life. Maybe there was nothing at all, no feeling, no responsibility toward anyone that allowed him to blow a man's head off.

And why always the head?

Was it because the target was smaller, more challenging?

Cannon supposed that it was something just that simple, a small target, a challenge to Creel and nothing more.

He slept and then there was an hour and a half layover while he changed trains and Cannon got a shave and a good breakfast and had time for a bath. At the depot he picked up a newspaper and read an article by Fred Sheridan; the man had a way with words, and he could see where Sheridan had once inflamed Price Shatlock to the point where Shatlock had to hire Creel to get rid of him.

The train swayed along, wheels clattering over the rail joints. A drummer across the aisle said, "Do you know that you can count the clicks of the wheels and time them and tell the exact speed of the train?" He consulted his watch and cocked his head a moment. "We are going exactly forty-two miles an hour." Then he snapped his fingers and brought the conductor down the aisle. "My good man," the drummer said, "may I inquire as to our speed?"

"About forty miles an hour," the conductor said.

The drummer beamed and the conductor scowled and went on down the aisle.

"Mathematics is my strong point," the drummer said. "We all have certain points that are stronger than others. Unfortunately, most men never realize what they are and thereby miss golden opportunities."

"You don't say," Cannon said.

"Mathematics is based on observation," the drummer said. "Allow me to introduce myself; Harry Fellows." Cannon gave the man his name, but he didn't think Fellows cared about it or would remember it. "Yes, correct answers depend on correct information through observation," Fellows went on. "Now I would say that you're a law officer."

Cannon showed his surprise. His coat was buttoned and his badge had never been revealed. He said, "Tell me why you think so. You've seen me before?"

"Never laid eyes on you until you got on the train," Fellows said, laughing softly. He was a young, pleasant man with a slightly brassy manner, yet he was a likeable man, a natural salesman. "If I reveal my methods, will you admit truthfully whether I'm right or wrong?"

"Sure," Cannon said, and crossed his legs and put his hands on his knees.

"Well," Fellows said, "first there are your boots. Obviously you ride a great deal, which first suggested that you were a cattleman. But I notice by the heels where you walk a great deal. Naturally this rules out working cattle; as you know, a real cattleman wouldn't walk from the bunkhouse to the corral. So we are faced with a job that requires mounted and dismounted work; a lawman suggests itself, but is in no way final. Then we have your suit, good, not expensive, but a little out of the average man's reach. Again, a deputy's pay. I notice by the bulges under your coat that you are heavily armed. And your hands, they are tough, but not rope-scarred. Again, a lawman; you can see where I automatically rule out the business trades. So I conclude that you are a lawman, and married." He raised an eyebrow, and smiled. "Right?"

"Right on both counts," Cannon said.

"A deputy?"

"Texas Ranger."

Harry Fellows frowned, then immediately brightened. "Well, I suppose a man can just get so close and that's that. If you don't mind my telling you, I deduced that you were a married man because you have a well-curried look about you that bachelors lack. Obviously some time ago a woman has brought you to a halter broke state."

Jim Cannon tipped his head back and laughed. "You're pretty good."

"Only pretty good?" Fellows pretended to pout. "Mr. Cannon, I am superb and I rarely make mistakes."

"What's your line?"

"I'm a purchasing agent for the railroad. My travels take me up and down and across Texas, and I enjoy every minute of it."

Jim Cannon thought a moment, then said, "Mr. Fellows, I wonder how much you can tell about a man who once had possession of an article."

"Try me," Fellows said. "Of course, one can tell more if the article was used for some time, years perhaps."

Cannon reached under his coat and pulled his gun and emptied it before handing it over to Harry Fellows. "A man gave me that. What can you tell about him?"

"I'll be frank, disregarding the fact that he may have been close to you. I say, may have been, because a man rarely gives up his firearm when he is still alive."

"He's dead," Cannon said.

Fellows looked at the bone-handles, examined the gun carefully, and even took the grips off with his pen-knife, using it as a screwdriver. Then he handed it back. "He was a slightly vain man, left-handed, and now and then broke. He was also careless with his things."

"You're right," Cannon said. "How?"

Harry Fellows shrugged. "Old rust pits on the cylinder could only mean prior neglect. The hammer is worn as only a left-handed man would wear it, and there are three sets of initials scratched inside the grips, indicating that it had been sold and bought back several times." He smiled. "The vanity part is a guess, because most men like walnut grips."

"I'm going to Kansas to conduct an investigation on two men," Cannon said. "Both men will be absent, and I couldn't offer you anything but the challenge, but—"

"Say no more," Fellows said, holding up his hand. "You've touched me at my weakest point; I would dearly love to test my talents. I get so few chances to use them other than for my own amusement." He laughed. "I'm going to visit my sister in Kansas City and the delay means nothing to me." He slapped his leg. "I may pick up a choice conversational piece here."

He offered Cannon a cigar and a moment later moved across the aisle.

It was, for Jim Cannon, a most enjoyable train trip.

Chapter Nine

Jim Cannon found Harry Fellows to be a very interesting man. College-educated, he had been in poor health and had gone first to Arizona where the climate was hot and dry, and then when he felt better, he migrated to Texas and got a job with the railroad; he had no intention of ever going back east to live.

They arrived in Ashland the next morning and checked in at the hotel, then got a shave before breakfast. Fellows had a way about him, a manner of speaking to the waiter that brought quick service. Cannon watched him for they were not alike; Fellows knew how to wear his clothes, how to handle himself smoothly, quickly having his way and making everyone like it.

After they ate, they walked along the street to the newspaper office and went in. A printer's devil whistled as he worked in the back room, and a gray, thin man sat at his desk and wrote with a slow, deliberate hand.

He looked up, then put his pencil down and came to the counter. "Can I help you?"

Cannon showed him his badge and said, "I'd like to ask you some questions."

"If I know the answers. My name is Hendricks. Ed Hendricks."

Cannon introduced himself, and Harry Fellows;

143

they all shook hands briefly then Hendricks looked inquisitively at Cannon. "I've lived here a good many years, and a newspaper man is supposed to know everything."

Cannon took a small notebook from his shirt pocket, and a pencil. "I'd like to know whether or not Sheriff Henry left town for any period of time during the last month and a half."

"Well, he's in Texas now and—" He looked sharply at Cannon. "Is this connected?" He grunted softly and made a wry face. "Well, it's not my business, other than to report it. I may make a few notes of my own."

"I'd as soon you didn't publish this in your paper just yet," Cannon said. "Now about the question."

"Well, Owen does take a week or two off now and then," Hendricks said, "but he never overdoes it. You know what I mean? He stays on the job and people don't mind a man going fishing once in awhile."

"During the last month and a half?"

Hendricks thought. "Now it seems to me he was gone, and had been back a day or two. Then he got the telegram from the rangers. Yes, he was gone about six days." He frowned. "Say, what's going on in Texas anyway? We heard McKitrick was arrested. Seems a little silly, a man like that. I'm saying this kindly, but Moss isn't what you'd call a violent man. Some ten, fifteen years ago he

144

had some trouble, shortly after he came to town to live. Fists flew, but he didn't do much fighting back. Took a pretty good beating and then sued. Didn't win it though; the judge threw it out of court."

"Maybe I could talk to this fella McKitrick fought," Cannon said. Then a thought came to him, an inspiration, a lesson he had learned from Harry Fellows, to observe, to analyze, to eliminate the improbabilities, and to act on the result, no matter how unlikely. "But of course I couldn't do that," Cannon said. "He's been dead for years."

"How did you know that?" Hendricks said, surprised.

"Could I look at your account of it in your file?"

"I'll find it," Hendricks said. "Be a minute or two."

He turned to the back room and Harry Fellows looked at Cannon. "You made a guess there, Jim. Want to tell me how?" Cannon quickly filled him in with Colonel Lavery's account of how Tass Creel had killed the sergeant, and Fellows smiled. "Good deduction there. The man would follow a pattern all right. If McKitrick is Creel—"

He stopped talking as Hendricks came back with a thick sheaf of bound newspapers. "Here it is, nearly fourteen years ago." He turned the whole thing around so Cannon and Fellows could read. "It was a tragic accident," Hendricks was

145

saying. "Tom Brady was a pretty well-liked man. A tough man, mind you; he was either for you or against you, and he just never hit it off with Moss McKitrick."

Cannon looked up from his reading. "It says here that Brady was killed when the steam boiler on his well drilling rig blew up. Did anyone find out how it happened?"

Hendricks shook his head. "He was alone at the time, in the early morning; it took better than an hour and a half to work up the pressure. His hired man hadn't arrived yet, but he heard the explosion. The safety valve must have stuck. Who could tell from the scattered pieces? Brady was scalded like a chicken."

"Sure was a sad accident," Cannon admitted. "Where does Owen Henry live?"

"Two blocks south and one to your left."

Cannon turned to the door, then stopped, "And Moss McKitrick?"

"Why, right next door," Hendricks said.

"Thank you," Cannon said and went out. As he walked down the street, Harry Fellows sided him, glanced at him, but said nothing until they turned down a residential street.

"You know how to ask questions," Fellows said. "What can you tell me about Hendricks?"

"Why not much, I guess. I didn't think to notice."

"You must always notice everything," Fellows

admonished gently. "He's married and has a grandchild by a married daughter. He's a staunch Mason and fought on the wrong side in the war. At least wrong for Kansas. He had his teeth pulled within the last year, and he rides a bay horse."

Cannon stopped and stared. "All right now——"

"Simple. There was a child's picture and a young woman's picture in a frame on his desk. He's too old to be the husband, so logically he's the grandfather. I assumed the daughter because a man usually doesn't keep the daughter-in-law's picture. The Masonic emblem on his watch fob, and the ring; two adornments?" He laughed and shook his head. "The war? A regimental picture, all in gray. Did you notice how he kept lifting the bottom plate with his tongue? That would indicate that they still bothered him a little; it usually takes a man a year or so to get used to false teeth."

"You're just in the wrong business," Cannon said frankly.

"I'm pretty happy with my work," Fellows said.

The sheriff's house was not difficult to find, and it sat on a corner, with a vacant lot separating it from Moss McKitrick's house.

Cannon knocked and a large, gaunt woman answered the door. "Yeah, what do you want?"

"Mrs. Henry, I hate——"

"I ain't Mrs. Henry," she said quickly. "I'm Mrs. Sweeny, the housekeeper. What do you want? The sheriff ain't here."

"I know that," Cannon said. He produced the search warrant, and explained the purpose of it. She eyed him suspiciously, her arms crossed over her breasts.

"Makes no difference to me. I'm goin' to tell the deputy; this is his business." She stepped aside so they could go in, then snatched up a shawl and went on down the street, her step lively.

"A sound argument for bachelorhood there," Fellows said and stepped into the parlor for a look around. "This is going to be difficult. By that I mean that most everything has Mrs. Sweeny's touch. Perhaps, in Henry's room—"

"I'll look around," Cannon said and went into the rear of the house. The kitchen was orderly, and he looked into a back pantry and a bedroom which was obviously Mrs. Sweeny's, then he went back down the hall to the front of the house just as the front door burst open and Mrs. Sweeny pointed an accusing finger at him.

"That's the fella I told you about!"

The deputy, a young, impetuous man, brushed past her and made a quick advance toward Cannon, a hand under his coat where it was close to his pistol. "Let's see your identification, mister."

Cannon opened his coat and displayed his badge, then Fellows stepped from the parlor and said, "What's going on?"

His voice, so unexpected, surprised the deputy

and he jerked his gun and swung around and Cannon kicked out, catching him on the wrist. The .38 flew out of his hand and skidded on the floor and Harry Fellows picked it up and ejected the cartridges.

"You're jumpy," Cannon said, his voice soft. He nodded toward the parlor and the deputy went in, but kept his eyes on Cannon. After showing him the search warrant, the deputy's manner changed. "Been in this business long?" Cannon asked casually.

"About eight months," the man said. "I'm Bert Connors. Could I have my gun back?" He looked at Fellows, who glanced at Cannon, then handed it over. Connors holstered it without reloading it. "How come you want to look around here?"

"Just a routine investigation," Cannon said. "We're going next door after we're through here. Are McKitrick's boys at home?"

The deputy shook his head. "They're livin' at the farm. Been there nearly a year. They only come home on the weekends and none now that their ma and pa are gone. When's McKitrick and Sheriff Henry coming back?"

"I couldn't say." Cannon glanced at Mrs. Sweeny. "Where's the sheriff's room?"

"He has the whole upstairs to himself," she said.

"We'll take a look now, if you don't mind," Cannon said.

"Wouldn't do any good if I did," she said. "Just

don't leave things all tore up like those other fellas did."

Cannon had started up the stairs, but he stopped and turned and looked at her. "What other fellas?"

"About a month or so ago," she said. "Someone broke in here while the sheriff was gone. It was on a weekend and I was stayin' with my sister. Tore the sheriff's rooms up somethin' terrible. I wrote him a letter, tellin' him what had happened, and by golly, it happened again. Wednesday nights I go to prayer meetin' and when I come home the place had been busted into and things was scattered about. Sheriff Henry he came home a couple of days later and he was fit to be tied. Ain't that right, deputy?"

"He was foamin' at the mouth, that's for sure."

"I don't suppose," Harry Fellows asked, "you noticed any strangers in town about that time." He looked at Bert Connors.

"There may have been," Connors said. "Never thought to ask around though. Figured kids did it. Sheriff Henry's clamped down on some of their foolishness and I just figured they was gettin' back at him."

Cannon seemed satisfied and started up the stairs again, then he turned back. "Mrs. Sweeny, when you wrote the letter, where did you send it?"

"Why, Eagle Pass, Texas," she said. "Sheriff

Henry hailed from that country a long time ago and now and then goes back there."

"Thank you," Cannon said and went on up the stairs behind Harry Fellows. At the top landing, Fellows turned his head and grinned.

"I like that, what you do. You know, acting like you're all through then springing back. It's good, especially when you want a quick, honest answer before they have a chance to think."

They went into a room that contained a bed and two dressers and a marble topped wash stand. Fellows opened the closet door and looked and pawed the clothes hanging there, then he went to the dresser and carefully went through it.

Cannon found an old Sharps carbine, long in disuse for the Maynard tape primer mechanism was rusted badly. He found a Colt cap and ball pistol, the kind the Confederates used, and some yellowed tintypes of cavalrymen.

There were no letters, no papers of any kind, and no other photographs. Cannon sat down on the bed, his manner dejected. "Certainly not much here," he said. "We know he fought for the south, but what the hell good is that?"

"The thing that bothers me most," Harry Fellows said, "is that I haven't run across one single copy of the Eagle Pass paper. You did tell me that he subscribed to it, didn't you?"

"By God!" Cannon said and sprang from the bed. They went on with their search, and it was most thorough, and when they were through they went downstairs and found Mrs. Sweeny in the kitchen.

Fellows asked, "How many years has the sheriff been a widower?"

She showed her surprise. "Six now. They'd been married less than a year. A young thing she was, a flower, delicate."

"We're through here," Fellows said. "Thank you for the hospitality."

She grunted something and turned her back to them and they went out and started across the vacant lot. Cannon said, "What made you think he'd been married?"

"Think? I was certain. The suits, some hardly worn, but all gathering dust. A man dresses like that when he courts a woman. Then too there was no picture of her, nothing to remind him of her; some men find memory painful. I venture to say they occupied the downstairs of the house but since her death he moved upstairs. You noticed that the other two rooms were pretty much catchalls?"

Deputy Bert Connors was waiting on McKitrick's porch with a key. He got up when they approached and said, "Been waitin' for you. Find anything?"

"Nothing of value," Fellows said.

The deputy looked at him carefully. "Say, are you one of them Pinkerton fellows?"

"Shrewd of you," Fellows said and motioned toward the lock.

The deputy let them in and stood in the hall; the house had a musty, closed up smell. Cannon went into the parlor and let up the front shades so some light came into the room. There was a pump organ in the corner and oval framed pictures on the walls; her relatives.

Cannon said, "You don't have to stick around, deputy."

The man hesitated, then laid the key on the table. "Lock up and drop it around to the office when you're through. It's the only skeleton key we got."

He went out and closed the door and Cannon put his hands on his hips, not sure where to start. They went through the house carefully, then went out in back to the small barn and tool shed. There was an old buggy and harness, and some garden tools and a workbench in one corner and underneath it a box of tools.

"This is really a man's domain," Harry Fellows said. "A house usually has a woman's touch everywhere and it clouds up my judgment."

Cannon sat down on a sawhorse and watched Fellows prod about; the man was in everything and nothing seemed too insignificant for him to investigate. He spent some time examining one of the pine uprights for it was scarred and rounded at chest level, as though some beaver had gnawed it.

Cannon was growing impatient, but Harry Fellows seemed most interested. He looked at all the tools and placed a few on the bench; he looked at the buggy and the coiled whip on the far wall and all the harness, and even crawled into the loft and stayed there for fifteen minutes.

Then he came back and sat down beside Cannon and offered a cigar. When they were lighted, he said, "If I didn't know better, I would swear that two men lived in this house. One man, and I'm sure the one everyone sees and knows, is a quiet, family man, quite proper in his actions and words."

"And the other one?"

"He is insane," Fellows said simply, and it gave his pronouncement a terrible sincerity. He pointed to the upright with the curiously rounded section. "That baffled me for a time until I examined the whip coiled over there on the wall. Jim, the man I'm talking about stood here for perhaps an hour at a time and whipped that post. Crazy as that may sound, I can offer no other explanation. Now a normal man gets drunk, fights, cusses, or pouts, but an insane man, unable to focus his rage on the cause, will turn to something else, some other object and get rid of his rage in unusual ways." He puffed gently on his cigar. "Jim, if you wanted to catch a mouse, how would you do it?"

Cannon frowned. "Why, I'd put some cheese on a trap and cock it."

"What kind of a trap?"

"The kind you buy in the store, with a spring on it."

"Why not drown the mouse? Starve him?" Fellows asked.

"Aw fer Christ's sake," Cannon said, "who wants to fart around killing a mouse?"

"A man who's mentally unbalanced," Fellows said mildly. "Jim, you ought to take a look in the loft. Why don't you?" He motioned toward the ladder and Cannon went on up, with Harry Fellows behind him. At first he saw nothing, then he spotted the wire cage. It had been cleverly built, with an ingenious trapdoor and the bait inside. When the trapdoor fell, the bait was pulled out of reach and the mouse was imprisoned without food or water.

On the floor of the cage there were several tiny bits of bone.

"Can you visualize this, Jim? This small animal trapped, dying slowly from thirst and hunger, and this man, watching it daily. Look here. There's a box. See how the wood is polished where he sat for hours. Look at the cigar stubs and matches where he smoked while he waited, watching the bright, frightened eyes in this little animal. And over here, in this tin. There are soda crackers and some dried cheese there. He must have felt enjoyment eating while something starved."

"Good God," Cannon said softly.

"I'm not through," Fellows said. "Look over here." He led Cannon to another corner where a large porcelain basin sat. The water marks were plainly evident although most of it had evaporated. Leading to the pan was a small round ramp and near the top it was hinged and fastened to a spring. There was dried grease on the sharply down-sloping ramp and around the edge of the basin.

"Do you see how it worked? The ramp and basin were thickly greased and the basin was filled with water, deep enough so that the mouse, once in there, could not stand or climb out. The bait was placed past the trip and in getting it, the mouse went down the chute and into the water. And there the poor little devil swam, Jim, until its strength was gone and it drowned. Can you see him watching that?"

"It makes you want to throw up," Cannon said. "I've faced some killers, some men pretty fast with a six-shooter, and I was scared, but they didn't make me sick. Is that all up here?"

"It's enough," Fellows said and followed Jim Cannon down the ladder.

"These items I laid on the bench," Fellows said, pointing to them, "are something I'm sure are important, but I can't quite summon the mechanical ingenuity to put them together."

"Let me have a look," Cannon said.

He examined the pieces with care; they were

parts of some device, and he tried fitting one against the other and for ten minutes he experimented, then he laughed.

"Sure, that's it." Quickly he sorted pieces and screws and when he was through he had a reloading tool, one that would size the spent cases, insert the primers and crimp the case around the bullet.

"Did you see anything that looked like a bullet mould?" Cannon asked.

"Is that what that was?" Fellows asked and dug into the tool box and came up with three pieces which Cannon quickly screwed together, attaching the sprue cutter last.

"That's a damn good mould," he said. "Forty-five caliber, and about four hundred and fifty grains. A .45-70 rifle for sure, since the Colt cartridge and Smith & Wesson are a lot lighter. See if you can find a scale. You have to weigh the powder, you know."

Fellows finally found it under the seat of the buggy, a delicate instrument that would finely measure the exact weights of bullet, and powder.

"I've always wondered whether Tass Creel rolled his own cartridges or not," Cannon said. "The factory stuff is good and reliable, but for the kind of shooting Tass Creel does, he'd have to take all the unpredictables out of it. He'd have to shoot fodder that was exactly the same every time or he couldn't call his shots so close."

"You realize," Fellows said, "that all this is not really evidence at all. It merely shows that Moss McKitrick is an unbalanced man who now and then loads .45-70 cartridges."

"I know that," Cannon said. "But it makes me more sure of myself."

"Did you get what you came here for?"

"Yes, and no. I wanted proof. I didn't get that."

"You haven't eliminated the sheriff then?"

"Yes, I have. As Tass Creel I have. But the captain won't. He's a lawyer and likes proof. So does the judge."

"Let's go back to the house," Fellows said. "We still haven't found something which I think is vital."

Cannon grinned. "The newspapers? Look in the upstairs hall closet. They've got Henry's name on them but it figures what's happened. Henry gives them to McKitrick after he's through reading them."

Harry Fellows laughed heartily. "You *are* coming along. Very well. And as you told me on the train, it rather solves the question of how McKitrick, if he is Creel, could get those Uncle Charlie notices so readily."

"The trouble is, every question we answer raises another we can't answer." He sighed. "I'm ready to lock it up. You?"

"Yes," Fellows said.

They closed up the house and started down the

street, then Cannon laughed softly. When Fellows looked at him, he said, "I was just thinking of what that green deputy said about you being a Pinkerton man."

Fellows put his hand into his breast coat pocket and brought out a folder. "I hate to give you a red face, Jim, but—"

Cannon stopped and looked at the identification then swore good naturedly. "Damn it, why didn't you say so before?"

Fellows returned the identification folder to his pocket. "Well now what kind of a detective would I be if I told everyone who I was? But I was telling you straight when I said I was going to visit my sister. Even I like a little time off once in awhile."

"By God, you owe me supper," Cannon said.

"That's a deal," Fellows said and they went on down the street.

Chapter Ten

That evening Harry Fellows caught the eastbound train, but Jim Cannon stayed on in Ashland; he wasn't through nosing around. The two men said goodbye and parted and Cannon stood on the platform until the train was out of sight, feeling that in this short period of time they had become good friends.

He took a room at the hotel, then sat on the porch, waiting for the deputy; he knew he would come, for lawmen are a clannish lot and like to spend a lot of time with one another.

The deputy came along and stopped and they talked for better than an hour and Cannon kept steering the conversation, dropping his questions easily, making most of them a mistaken statement that had to be corrected.

Finally the deputy had to get on with his rounds and after he walked on down the street, Jim Cannon walked on down to the depot and the telegrapher's office. The man was alone, reading a magazine, waiting for a dead wire to come alive; he looked up as Cannon came in.

"Want to send a wire," Cannon said.

"You want to write it or tell me?" the man asked.

"I'll write it." He drew a blank to him and then thought of the wording. There was no use taking the chance that the telegrapher was a talker and spreading a lot of gossip around town. He worded his message carefully:

N. Eiler
Texas Battalion
Rock Springs, Texas
True identity of prisoner no longer in doubt.
We were right. Returning first southbound.
Newest suspect once resident of Eagle Pass.
Have Pine check.

Cannon

He paid for the wire and stood there while the telegrapher sent it and got an all clear, then Cannon went to the hotel. There was a time in his life when a night in a strange town meant no sleep at all, but he was past that foolishness now and went to his room and undressed for bed.

A knock woke him and he lit the lamp and looked at his watch; he had been asleep for nearly two hours. He pulled on his pants and went to the door and found the deputy there.

"You go to bed early," he said.

"I get up early," Cannon said. "What did you want?"

The deputy stepped inside and took off his hat. "You know, it bothered me, what you said about me not checking after the sheriff's house was busted into. So I've been asking around. Kind of tough, with so much time gone by, but I did find out a few things that might help."

"Like what?" Cannon asked.

"Some fellas was seen in town, strangers." He held up three fingers and added, "Two came together; one came alone. The two that came together, Barnstalk at the store remembered because one came inside and asked directions while the other stayed outside. Barnstalk thought that was peculiar, but then, he thinks most everything is peculiar."

"Could he describe 'em?"

"Elderly gents pretty well dressed. The one who came inside talked like he run things pretty much to suit himself all his life." The deputy grinned. "He got a little short with Barnstalk, and he don't like that."

"Keene and Maybry," Cannon said as though talking to himself.

The deputy's eyes widened. "Do you know 'em?"

"I know of 'em," Cannon said. "And the third man?"

"Well, pretty sketchy there, except that the station agent remembered him gettin' off the train and askin' where Henry lived. Elderly too, well-dressed."

"Whitlow," Cannon said. "Well I'll be damned. They wanted to hire Creel too."

"It sure don't make any sense to me," the deputy

said, turning to the door. "Sorry to have woke you."

"That's all right," Cannon said and closed the door. He thought for a moment, then dressed and went back to the telegraph office; Nathan Eiler would appreciate this bit of information when he questioned Whitlow again. He worded his wire, sent it, then walked back toward the hotel. The saloon was open and noisy and he went inside, thinking that a glass of beer might make him sleepy. He knew no one so he stepped up to the bar and laid a dime in front of him. The bartender saw this and drew a large beer and slid it his way.

He let himself be surrounded by the buzz of talk and the sound of the gay piano as though he were an island. No one spoke to him and he did not intrude on anyone. He thought about the single days when he used to hit the saloon as soon as he reached town, not because he had a burning thirst, but because there were people there.

I was like a dog chasing its tail, he thought and sipped his beer. Cannon paid no attention at all to who came in or out of the place, and when the bartender came up to him and asked, "You the Texas Ranger?" he was surprised. He nodded and watched the bartender walk the length of the bar and speak to a pair of young men there.

They came around the end and walked down

toward Cannon and the oldest, who was big for sixteen, did the talking. "I'm Wyley McKitrick. Heard you were in town snooping around."

"Is that what you call it?" Cannon asked. The room quickly grew quiet; even the piano stopped. "What's on your mind, son?"

"When are you goin' to let Pa come home?" He had bold round eyes in a moon face and thin, compressed lips, and he stood with his hands in his mackinaw pockets.

"It isn't up to me to say," Cannon said softly. "Why don't you boys go back to the farm and let this work itself out?"

"We was thinkin' that maybe the State of Texas would like to swap you for Pa," Wyley said. "Do you suppose that would work?"

"You'd just get hurt," Cannon told him. "Ain't your pa got enough trouble without you mixing some more for him?"

"It's all a mistake," Wyley McKitrick said. "You'll see."

"Then you have nothin' to worry about," Cannon said. "He'll be home soon."

"That ain't good enough. We want him home now."

"Boy, we can't always have what we want, now can we?" He looked past Wyley; the other boy was standing slightly back, his eyes steady on Cannon. Of the two boys, he was clearly the true chip off the old block; the similarity struck

Cannon sharply and the idea came to him, completely developed.

Cannon said, "Why don't you boys go home, throw some clothes in a suitcase, and come back with me and see your pa? He'd like that and you could all come home together."

"I—Wyley—" He looked at his brother. The suggestion had thrown them off balance.

Reaching out, Cannon pulled Wyley's hand from his pockct and squeezed the wrist and made him drop the nickel-plated .32 on the bar. "Using that would only get you in a lot of trouble," he said. "Now why don't you do as I say? It's better that way."

The bartender said, "He's right, boys. Your pa'd like that."

Cannon supposed it was the familiar voice that did it, the boys hesitated, then nodded and went out and afterward the bartender sighed with relief. "You ran a good bluff there. They won't get steam up to try it again."

"Did you think I was bluffing?" Cannon asked. He finished his beer, scooped up the .32 and dropped it in his pocket and went out. Before he went to his room he told the clerk to get two train tickets and tack them onto the bill, then he went up the stairs.

The bed was comfortable; this was a first-rate hotel, and he slept well, waking when the first touch of daylight came through his open window.

He washed and shaved and then went down to get his breakfast.

The McKitrick boys were in the lobby, asleep in the chairs and he woke them. "Let's get something to eat on the State of Texas," he said. A pause at the desk to sign the bill and pick up the tickets and he joined them on the street.

They went into a small restaurant near the depot and ordered; there was no one in the place except the counterman and a negro fry cook. While they ate, Wyley said, "What did you mean, the State of Texas payin' for this?"

"Mmm?" Cannon laughed. "Well, we move around considerable and if we had to pay all our own hotel bills, food bills, and horse keep, we'd go in the hole. The state gives us so much a day for meals and board. We ride the trains for free. If we need a horse, we rent one and the state pays for it. It costs a lot of money to catch lawbreakers, boy. Sometimes thousands of dollars." He bent forward and looked at Burgess. "Don't he ever talk?"

"He never has much to say," Wyley said. "He don't get in much trouble either."

"One has a lot to do with the other," Cannon admitted.

It came train time and they went to the depot and when the train pulled into the station and stopped, they got aboard. Cannon waited until they were forty miles out of Ashland, waited until they were used to the idea of traveling, then he excused himself and went forward into the next car and found the conductor there. He produced his credentials and got the conductor's attention.

"I'd like to send a wire to be dropped off at the first telegraph station you come to."

The conductor checked his watch. "Fifteen minutes. It can go off with the mail sack. I'll get you a blank."

Cannon waited in the drafty vestibule and when the conductor came back with the blank he wrote holding it against the steel end of the coach.

N. Eiler
Frontier Battalion
Rock Springs, Texas
Lavery unable to identify suspect because of changes through years. Will arrive early afternoon tomorrow with spitting image of suspect at age fifteen. Some new ideas on case I wish to discuss.

Cannon

He gave the message to the conductor and stood in the vestibule until the train slowed. Then he leaned out and saw the message passed on to a man standing in the cinders by a yellow shack; the train picked up speed and Cannon went back to his coach.

. . .

Judge Rainsford sat in the deep leather chair, his head tipped forward so far that his chin almost touched his chest; he held a glass of whiskey and he seemed asleep, but he was not. Colonel Lavery liked the hardbacked chair; he was a product of a spartan military life and could not shake lifelong habits. Eiler was at his desk and Jim Cannon sat in the other leather chair, one leg crossed over his knee.

"Are you certain?" Rainsford said. "Colonel, a man dare not make a mistake in a thing like this."

"In the moment I saw him," Lavery said, "thirty years rolled away and I was back to the siege of Atlanta." He turned his head and glanced at Jim Cannon. "Put Moss McKitrick's son in Union blue and you have Tass Creel. No, there's no mistake now. The weight McKitrick had put on, the thinning hair, all added up to change him so that I couldn't be sure. But to see that boy—"

"Then we're in agreement that we have our man," Eiler said. "Judge?"

"We may have him to *our* satisfaction," Rainsford said, "but as a jurist I would have to honestly say that if you brought him to my court and presented the case you have, I'd throw it out. A strong net of circumstantial evidence has been woven about McKitrick, but there is not one solid fact in the whole lot of it. You need a witness who can point his finger and say, 'Yes, that's Tass Creel.'"

"Jim, you haven't said much, and I know you well enough to know that you're bustin' to say something." Eiler looked at him.

"It's pretty wild," Cannon said.

"Let's hear it," Rainsford suggested.

Cannon talked while he rolled a smoke. "From Colonel Lavery's account we pretty well agree that Tass Creel's a little crazy. All right, from what I found out in Ashland, you'll have to agree that McKitrick's crazy too. I'm just beginning to find out how little I know about criminals, but it sure seems to me that Creel has been pretty successful in leading two lives. One part of Creel is Moss McKitrick, pillar of the church and family man. But we know now that there are times when the Tass Creel part just cries to bust out. One half of him has a family and a home and sons. What's the other half have? It don't seem to me that the Creel half would take a back seat."

"What are you suggesting?" Lavery asked.

Rainsford brightened. "That Tass Creel has a family, a home somewhere," he said, snapping his finger. "Damn it, Eiler, why isn't this man a sergeant at least?" He got up and began to pace up and down the office. "Of course, of course, it makes complete sense."

Nathan Eiler said, "That's quite an idea, Jim. Quite an idea indeed. But where do we start?"

169

"I don't know," Cannon said. He took a final puff on his smoke then got up to crush it out in Eiler's ashtray. "Captain, did you ever clear up who knifed Knapsack?"

"No," Eiler said. "Not a clue." He looked at Cannon. "And we haven't found Charlie Dixon either."

Cannon remained by Eiler's desk. He said, "Captain, a man told me that if one thinks over a problem carefully and removes all the impossibilities, then whatever remains, strange as it may be, has to be the right answer."

"I wouldn't argue with that," Eiler said. "But what's it got to do with Knapsack or Charlie Dixon?"

Cannon scratched his head. "Jack didn't know anyone here. Except the one who killed him, and that narrows the field down to Creel, Whitlow, and Charlie Dixon."

"Creel was in a cell," Eiler said.

"And Whitlow hadn't been here yet," Eiler said.

"So that leaves Charlie Dixon. Like Creel, we don't know Dixon on sight, but he knew Knapsack and killed him before he could talk."

"I don't exclude the possibility that Dixon might have been in town," Eiler said.

"No, sir, but I thought about that too. What's Dixon doin' in town? I suppose we could safely figure because he wanted to see Price Shatlock die. But why would he stay around? The job was done. He had his revenge. Then I ask myself what are the chances of him meeting Knapsack so far from Wyoming. And add to that the off chance that they'd be in town on the same night, run into each other, so to speak." He shook his head. "Captain, this Charlie Dixon is like Tass Creel; we know him by a different name."

Eiler waved his hand. "Don't we have enough to worry about without getting involved on this tangent?"

"Well, I think both trains run on the same track," Cannon said. "Dixon hired Creel to kill Shatlock."

"And according to your investigation," Eiler said, "so did Whitlow and the others. Or they tried." He rubbed a hand across his face. "Where in hell is Burke Pine anyway? The old coot's probably taking Spanish guitar lessons and drinking wine with some fat woman." He got up and went to his window and watched the sunset. "I want a confession from Moss McKitrick. A full confession."

"It might be," Cannon said, "that such a thing can be arranged."

Had he tendered his resignation he could not have drawn more attention; Eiler turned quickly and stared. "Keep talking," he said.

"Creel's insane. For my money, I'd work on that angle until he broke. It seems to me that he don't have too good a grip on what's real and what ain't as it is. If he could be mixed up he might trip himself up."

"How do you go about that?" Rainsford asked.

Cannon frowned. "Well, sir, I'd get a hotel room in town and fix it up with the kind of lamps he always used, then some night I'd take him in when it was pitch dark and sit him down. Then I'd uncover them lamps and let him face Whitlow just like he'd done in the past. And I'd put Sheridan there. Remember that Creel had him tagged for killing and missed. He may not know that Sheridan is alive."

"It has possibilities," Rainsford said.

"That ain't all, sir," Cannon said. "I'd put his wife and boys in that chair too, just like they was payin' him to kill someone."

Eiler, who knew Cannon well, said, "Who are they hiring him to kill, Jim?"

"Why, Moss McKitrick, of course."

"She'd never do it," Rainsford said. "To her own husband?" He shook his head vigorously. "Not a chance."

"How is she goin' to know it's him?" Cannon asked.

The idea seemed to appall Rainsford, but Eiler held up his hand. "Now wait a minute, judge. This whole thing has some merit. It needs refinement, but it's good. McKitrick may break under it. He would really break if we could produce Charlie Dixon."

172

"Don't leave me out of this," Lavery said. "Creel hates me. And coming from so far back in his past, it might stir him badly."

"If we could eliminate the woman—" Rainsford began, then shrugged. "Of course I'm thinking of legal repercussions if this backfires."

Eiler was taking hold of the idea. "I see exactly how this would have to be played. In every way we deny McKitrick the right to his Kansas identity. To everyone he is Tass Creel. He'll fight that. God knows the man must have waged a terrible battle through the years to preserve it."

"Jim," Rainsford said, "we're playing with a high explosive here. I do think it might be better, since we have gone this far in establishing, at least in our own minds, Creel's alternate identity, to turn him loose and wait our chance to catch him at work."

"No!" Eiler snapped. "Damn it, judge, I don't want to butt heads with you, but I'll fight that."

"I was only thinking of the alternatives," Rainsford said. "We can't prove a case against Creel or McKitrick. If this new scheme fails, we'll not only have to let him go but face a severe suit in civil court."

"Oh, to hell with that," Eiler said. "Sue and be damned. I'm after one of the worst killers the West has ever been plagued with and if the State of Texas is unhappy in the way I bring him to justice, let them terminate my commission." He blew out a long breath and calmed himself. "Jim, you might as well go home. I want you to arrange for the room at the hotel. Tomorrow night, around eleven. Take care of all the details. We'll bring Creel in the back way."

"All right, sir," Cannon said and went to the door. He started to open it, then said, "Oh, I think the judge had a good idea there, promoting me to sergeant."

"You're on the list," Eiler said, "but I might speed it along. Now get out of here."

Cannon grinned and closed the door and went outside. Fred Sheridan was sitting on the porch rail smoking a slim cigar. He said, "Long conference."

"I picked up a couple of good stories in Kansas," Cannon said.

Sheridan shrugged. "All right, so it's none of my business."

"The captain hands out news to the press around here," Cannon said. "How come you're holding the porch down?"

Sheridan pointed his cigar at the guardhouse. "Saw two boys and Mrs. McKitrick go in a half hour ago. I thought they might have something to say when they came out." He looked at Cannon. "Why did you bring the boys back with you?"

"They were lonesome for their pa."

"That's a touching bit of sentiment," Sheridan admitted.

"I read one of your articles on the train," Cannon said. "You don't have much use for anyone, do you?"

"The world's a tough place," Sheridan opined. "You get kicked around until it hurts. Once in a while I do some kicking of my own. Whitlow and the others, they deserve what Shatlock got. Legal or otherwise, I don't care."

"I can understand your point of view," Cannon said. "What was the name of that newspaperman friend of yours Creel killed? It seems to have slipped my mind."

"I never said."

"Tell me now then."

Sheridan hesitated, then said, "What does it matter? It was a long time ago."

Cannon did not press the point. "Tomorrow night we're havin' a party in town. You might say it's a command performance, so we just can't excuse any absence."

"I was thinking of going back to Dallas for a few days," Sheridan said. "What kind of a party?"

"The captain will explain it. We're throwin' this in honor of Tass Creel."

"That's a grisly joke, Cannon. Not funny at all."

"Well, I wasn't trying to be," Cannon said. "So postpone your trip, huh?"

"Generally I do what I want," Sheridan said. "It takes a good reason for me to break that rule."

Cannon laughed and tapped him on the arm.

"The captain is good at thinking of reasons, and this time I'd listen carefully to him."

He walked off the porch and went to the stable where he saddled up and rode out for town. At the gate he looked back and saw Sheridan still sitting on the porch railing.

Chapter Eleven

Burke Pine was the kind of free-spending tourist the cantina owners of Piedras Negras liked; he slept late, liked his night life, and bothered no one.

As soon as he arrived in Eagle Pass, he checked with the resident ranger and the city marshal, showed them the photo of Tass Creel and discovered that neither man had ever seen him before. The town was small and the residents permanent, so Pine took the photo around to the merchants and the telegrapher and got the same answer: none of them had ever seen Tass Creel before.

Pine decided to cross the river and have a look on the other side, and since he hadn't drawn much attention to himself, he thought he might do better if he left his badge behind and put his gun in his satchel.

For three days he had lived at the inn, spent considerable time in the cantinas, and generally was accepted as a nice *gringo* who didn't mind buying a drink for a man who was thirsty. In three days he became a familiar sight in the village, then Pine began to ride in the mornings and no one thought anything of it; every Mexican knew that the rich ride while the poor walk.

By the fifth day, Burke Pine had reached a

name-exchanging basis with every sheep-herding peon and every rancher in a ten-mile fan. Pine really did not know what he was looking for, but like any good peace officer, he felt that he would recognize any clue that came his way.

Twice, during his stay in Piedras Negras, Pine saw a man in town who aroused his curiosity. The poor were dirty and the rich were clean, and somewhere in between there were a few who were clean but obviously poor; these were the servants of the rich and Pine saw them in the markets every day. Yet this man he had only seen twice, and both times mounted, so he asked about him in a casual way and got his answer just as casually.

"Heem? He is Tomas, the servant of the *Rancho el Paso Negras*."

That answer was supposed to explain everything to him, and it didn't, but he figured to have a look at this rancho himself and asked no more about it. But the name itself gave him a pretty good idea where to look, because he already knew there was a mountain pass to the east, and a road of sorts.

A minor official from the local police threw a hitch into his plans when he came to the cantina and politely asked Pine to come along; the Mexicans were saddened for they understood this and suspected all along that Pine was a *bandito*; they knew the rich were either born that way or stole it; no man to their knowledge ever made it by toil.

At the river, Pine was turned over to two Texas Rangers, both personal friends of his, but in no way did they let on that they even knew him.

Bert Clinton was the resident ranger and in his office he handed over the wire Nathan Eiler had sent. "I can save you the trouble," Clinton said. "Henry used to own a ranch about eight miles north of here. Anthrax wiped him out."

"I don't recall him when I was here," Pine said. "But that was some years ago."

"He was long gone," Clinton said. "I never knew him, but there are plenty of older residents who do." He wrote a note to himself then put the pencil aside. "I'll check on it to make it official."

"Do you know where *Rancho el Paso Negras* is?" Pine asked.

Clinton frowned. "On the Mexican side?" He shook his head. "In the interests of good relations, I never go past the town, and when I do cross, I go only to the police station. But I could check it out—"

"No, no," Pine said quickly. "I'll take care of it. They don't pay any attention to me now. If you made an official move, it might fix me up good."

"All right," Clinton said. He smiled. "You can go back now. I'll drop a word to the police there that we only wanted to ask you a few questions about a robbery. How's the money holding out?"

"Let me have another hundred dollars," Pine said.

Clinton took it from a locked box in his desk. "Keep this up and taxes are goin' to get higher." He counted the money and Pine pocketed it and left.

He crossed the river again and went to the cantina and they celebrated his return; and he drank with them and got talkative and they all learned that the rangers didn't have a thing on him.

Everyone drank tequila on Burke Pine that night.

Early the next morning he left town and rode east with a pack burro and he kept riding that day and camped the night in the mountains. At dawn he was moving again, working up the steep pass and by midafternoon he reached the summit and started down toward a broad valley. He could see the buildings, the walled rancho in the distance.

Pine worried none at all about his reception, for he was a traveler and they were Spanish. With their traditions of hospitality, he could stay an hour or a month and there would be no questions asked.

All his looking and listening had earned him nothing; he had not picked up one solitary trace of Tass Creel in this area and he was beginning to wonder if he was ever going to. Captain Eiler's telegram urged him on, and it contained Jim

Cannon's suggestion that Creel had a home here. It was, Pine thought, worth looking into.

His approach to the gate was steady and in plain sight for the last four miles; a Mexican opened it and he rode in and dismounted by the watering trough. The yard fronting the house was a garden, for a good well provided water for the trees.

Pine drew some attention; any stranger would, and there was a man walking toward him, a squat, powerful Mexican with some silver on his jacket and a pearl-handled .44 at his side. The Mexican swept off his hat and said, "I am Jesus Pedro Alvarez, *señor.*" He waved his hand to indicate it all. "It is my honor to be the foreman of *Rancho el Paso Negras.*" He spoke in Spanish and Pine, born and raised to the language, answered him, introducing himself, and offering a casual excuse for being there. Alvarez was in his mid-thirties, and he would have been handsome had not a deep scar slashing his cheek twisted his features slightly.

He saw Pine's attention on the scar and he smiled. "I wear this with pride, *señor.* It was given to me by the *patron* himself to drive the young foolishness from me and put me to my work."

"A cut as deep as that must have been would drive anything out of a man," Pine said.

"I was twenty-three," Alvarez said. "My father, who was in charge of this rancho, died in a fall from his horse. The *patron* selected me to take his place, and I treated the responsibility too lightly. The *patron* is a man of iron, *señor*. A colonel in the army of the *Estados Unidos*."

Pine arched an eyebrow. "Is that a fact? I'd like to meet him. Been in the army myself, you know."

"I regret to say that the *patron* is not here," Alvarez said. "He is not given much leave, and usually is here no more than a month or so out of the year." He expanded a bit with pride. "I am happy to say that the *patron*, when he arrives, can find no fault with the *rancho*."

"That's some responsibility," Pine admitted. "How far does the rancho extend?"

"To the mountains on both sides and the entire length of the valley." He indicated the directions with his hand. "Many square miles, *señor*. When I was a young boy, this land was in the hands of bandits. Then the *patron* came here and killed the bandit leader. It was a great thing, for the *patron* did it alone. He killed many of the bandits and they left the country."

An inner excitement was building in Burke Pine, but he let none of it show on his face; he kept his manner friendly and relaxed, interested but not prying. "Your *patron* must be some tom turkey," he said. "Single-handed, you say? Must be an old Indian fighter. They knew how to handle themselves."

"I have not seen a finer shot with a rifle," Alvarez admitted. "From incredible distances, I have seen him bring down game. It was so with the bandit leader, Manuel Ortega."

Pine squinted and pursed his lips as though thinking hard. "Say, I've heard of an army officer who was that kind of a shot. Name of—ah—damn, but it escapes me now—"

"Henry Moss, *señor*. He is no doubt famous in the *Estados Unidos*."

"That's the fella," Pine said, nodding. "Well, I'll give my horse a drink, fill my canteen, and be on my way."

"You are welcome to remain at *Rancho el Paso Negras*," Alvarez said. "That is the wish of the *señora*." He bowed and put on his hat. "I will tell her you are here."

He walked briskly across the shaded yard and Pine gave his horse some water. While he was there at the well, the gates opened and a young man rode in on a splendid bay and when he saw Pine, he wheeled about and came over. He was young and stocky and although his hair was dark, his skin was light and his eyes blue.

With a flourish he dismounted and extended his hand. And he spoke English. "I'm Alfredo Moss. Welcome to *Rancho el Paso Negras*."

"Burke Pine. Met your foreman."

The young man smiled. "He is a great talker. No doubt he has told you much about the rancho. A fiercely proud man, *señor*. He would kill anyone or anything that meant harm."

"He looked like a man who could use his six-shooter," Pine said. Then he glanced at the brace of pistols young Moss wore. "Are you in the habit of being that well-armed?"

"Every man on the *rancho* is prepared to fight, should we be forced to," young Moss said. "That is the teaching of my father. To be strong, you must create a fortress of yourself. Have you been to the *hacienda*?"

"No," Pine said. "I just stopped to water my horse and fill my canteen."

"You have business on our land?"

"Passing through," Pine said. He had been studying the young man, watching the quick darting eyes, gauging the intelligence there, and he decided to play this straight. "I'm a Texas Ranger. You might even say, a Texas Ranger on business."

"There is no one on this *rancho* who has ever been across the river," Alfredo Moss said. "Your business is not here. But come. I'll take you to my mother. She will like to meet you."

They went together to the house and in the shade the air was cool; inside, the temperature dropped sharply for the adobe walls and the tile roof kept back the heat. The entranceway was a large hall and a servant came up immediately. Young Moss spoke to him in rapid Spanish, then said, "This way, please."

They went into a cool, low-ceilinged room, shaded from the sun, and he saw her then, a small, dark woman half hidden in a large chair. Alfredo Moss introduced Burke Pine, who knew exactly how to conduct himself in the presence of a lady; he took her hand and bent over it, brushing it more with his mustache than his lips. He spoke to her in Spanish, flattering her tastefully, and it pleased her, told her something about him, and she waved to a chair and indicated his welcome and acceptance.

Alfredo said, "*Señor* Pine is an officer in the Texas police."

She looked at him, her dark eyes attentive. She spoke in English. "Do your duties bring you to *Rancho el Paso Negras*?"

"Only in a small way," Pine said. "You speak English well. Surely you were taught in the *Estados Unidos*."

She laughed softly. "My husband taught me many years ago, after we were married. I did not speak a word of English and he spoke no Spanish, but we had the language of love. Do you know my husband, *señor*?"

"Indeed I do," Pine said. "You foreman told me that *Señor* Moss saved this land from bandits."

"It is a story Alvarez likes to tell," she said. "This land belonged to my father, but the bandits came and drove us away. I was a young girl at the time and we were forced to live in Piedras Negras.

My father was killed by the bandits. But there was a young officer from the army of the *Estados Unidos* in the village. He had talked to my father about the bandits, but I knew nothing of what was said because he was killed."

"I have heard this tale many times," Alfredo said. "My father's uniform was blue, with many buttons, and for a weapon he had a rifle as tall as a man, and so heavy that only he could carry it."

"That's some story," Pine said honestly.

"The *patron* was a man of great strength," Alfredo said. "He put fear in the heart of the bandits and they fled across the mountains and never returned."

His mother smiled. "Sit down and do not prattle." She turned to Burke Pine. "We were married then and he built the *rancho* as you see it."

"It's some ranch," Pine admitted. "You've been happy?"

"I could not be happier," she said. "He is away so much, but then he comes home and time does not pass quickly when he is here. He rules with a hand of iron, *señor*, but that is because he is an officer and knows no other way."

"You must visit him now and then," Pine suggested.

She shook her head. "I am happy here, and he has told me about the army. They would not accept me because I am Spanish, and I would not harm his career. Soon, this year, he will come to stay. His work in the army is ended. He told me this in a letter."

Burke Pine found it difficult to sit still and keep his poker face, but he knew that he had to. If he made one false move now, one thoughtless, hasty remark, he might see the whole thing fly out the window.

"When I last saw your husband, he expressed a wish that you would join him. I could," Burke Pine said casually, "arrange to take you to your husband. I know where he is."

"That's kind of you, but he would not like it," she said. "He is a firm man and through the years he has told me that our home is here, and that he will come to me." She studied him carefully. "I feel that you do not tell me everything."

"Well, I'm not a man to ruin another man's surprises," Pine admitted. "Your husband is no longer in the army, if that's a concern to you."

Alfredo Moss spoke excitedly. "I would like to go to the *Estados Unidos*."

"You are always wanting to go someplace," she chided. "I could not leave the *rancho*."

"It would be in good hands," Pine pointed out. "And I know your husband will be—well, surprised to see you."

"It is not easy to go against his wishes," she said. "He is not a man who likes to be disobeyed." Her attention sharpened. "You claim to know the *patron*. Describe him to me."

187

Pine closed his eyes and painted a word picture of Tass Creel, only he dressed him up a little and put a colonel's uniform on him. Then he waited.

Alfredo said, "He has described him to the letter. Can there be any doubt?"

"It is so," she said softly. "But why have I received no letter? You are a stranger to me, *señor*."

"But not to your husband," Pine said. He stood up. "I'm going to Piedras Negras and I'll wait three days, to give you time to think it over. But I might add that he could be angry because you didn't come to him this time. A man says one thing and hopes another, and loneliness can work on a man too."

"I will go with you to the gate," Alfredo said.

Pine was glad to be alone with the young man and as he untied his horse, he said, "You're a man, Alfredo. She is a woman. It will take a man to make the decision for her."

"That is true," he said. "You have done us a service, *señor*."

"Glad to," Pine said and rode back.

When he got to the village, he slept a few hours, then crossed the river and sent a long telegram to Captain Nathan Eiler, and he figured it would be worth at least a month's pay just to see Eiler's expression when he got it.

The noose around Tass Creel's neck was just about as tight as a man could draw it, Pine decided, and it had been a long run for him, a long and tiring run.

In his lifetime he had known a few men who had two wives at the same time and he often marveled that they even got away with it for a short time. A woman, by nature, was mighty suspicious, and for a man to be away for long periods of time just naturally went against their grain.

Then too, Creel's "wives" were so different. One was a dowdy frump with a nagging manner and the other was a grand lady whose Spanish blood ran clear for close to a thousand years. In one life Creel was a middle-class dirt farmer who liked to spend his time standing around with his hands tucked into the bib of his overalls, and in the other he was a hard ruler of a vast ranch empire.

But neither was real to Burke Pine. There was only one man: Tass Creel, a cold-blooded killer.

He made arrangements with the resident ranger for the train, then crossed the river again and spent his time sleeping. There was little doubt in his mind but what they would show up; he was staking everything on Alfredo, who was an only son and pretty well pampered. Alfredo would convince his mother and Pine counted on that.

It made sense to Pine now, the chase across the desert. Creel probably used that route after each job, watered up at the spring, then pushed east across the pass. And it made sense too why no one in Eagle Pass knew him; he simply never crossed the river. He stayed out of the village too, which would draw no attention for the ranch was quite a ways out and the rich always sent servants to do their bidding.

Smart, Pine admitted. Smart and rich. This struck him oddly for honest men worked hard all their lives to get enough to bury them and a man like Tass Creel could break every sacred rule in the book and end up with the fat of the land. But of course Pine realized that was relative; the man was going to be hung and he couldn't take it with him.

He was bothered too by the fact that he was going to have to ruin some innocent lives. Creel's Kansas wife would go to pieces; she was the kind who'd panic when a fly got caught in the cake batter. And Creel's Spanish wife, well, he couldn't figure that. She was a noble woman and they had a lot of inbred poise. She just might take it with her head high.

It perplexed him to think that these two women could have lived all these years with Tass Creel and never really known the genuine man. He was an actor playing three roles so cleverly that he never once got his lies mixed up.

A servant at the inn came to his room and told him that his party from *Rancho el Paso Negras* had arrived, and Pine dressed and went into the main room with his suitcase in hand. She had brought one servant to handle the luggage, and they went to the river without further delay. Two rangers came across with a wagon and took them to the station.

Alfredo wanted to see the town since they had nearly two hours until train time, but his mother would not permit it; she was still against the idea but torn between the will of two men and feeling pretty helpless about it.

"How long will the journey take?" she asked.

"Not long," Pine said. "Six hours."

"It must be the right thing, what I am doing." She fell silent and nursed her suspicions and doubts and the train finally came and they got aboard.

They rode in the day coach and Alfredo was too busy looking out the window to worry or to have any doubts, but they were written plainly in his mother's face.

"You know the *patron*," she said, "but you have not explained the circumstances. I would like to hear them." She sat across from him and demanded the truth, and it was a moment he had hoped would not come.

"I suppose all this has to come out sooner or later," Pine said. "But being a man who is weaker than I thought, I wanted to put the burden of it all on someone else. We have your husband in the stockade at Rock Springs. The charge is murder."

Alfredo lost all interest in the landscape. "That is a lie," he said.

"The truth," Pine said.

"A mistake," she said. "It must be!"

"No mistake," Pine said. She was steeling herself, so he gave it all to her in one big dose, while she was set for it. "The facts are, his name is Tass Creel, a professional killer."

"A lie!" Alfredo said.

Pine didn't even glance at him. "Creel has been living in Kansas under the name of McKitrick. He has a wife and two sons there."

"I will kill you for these lies!" Alfredo snapped and Burke Pine whipped his hand across the young man's mouth, knocking him back in the seat.

"Now sonny, you just sit there and keep your trap shut. I'm not going to have any trouble with you, and if you open your jaws once more I'll handcuff you in the baggage car. You understand that?"

"*Si.*"

"It's no pleasure to me to tell you these things, but they're goin' to have to be told, and I wouldn't be thanked for duckin' the job. Creel was never an officer in the United States Army. He was a renegade Union soldier. That's about the time you met him."

For a moment she stared, not speaking, then she said, "It is all the truth; I can see that in your eyes and hear it in your voice. You must be a brave man who has caught many dangerous men. Know then that you have taken a woman's heart and squeezed the blood from it."

"I'm sorry," Pine said. "I really am."

"Will that bring life to me now?" she asked and turned to look out the window.

She did not look at him again, not even when he helped her off the train at Rock Springs.

Chapter Twelve

Cannon found rooms for Creel's sons in town and arranged a pass from Eiler's office so that they could get in to see their father. Then he returned to Eiler's office. Rainsford and Lavery were there and Fred Sheridan sat with his chair tipped against the far wall.

Sheridan took his cigaret out of his mouth and said, "So what have you got, judge?"

"Nothing," Rainsford said. "We're satisfied personally, but any jurist would throw it all out. I need a confession. And the testimony of witnesses."

"You won't get a thing from George Whitlow," Sheridan said.

"It's like a loaded gun," Eiler said, "and we need something to trigger it off." He looked out the window. "Be dark in another two hours. Is everything ready at the hotel, Jim?"

"Yes, sir. Just as ready as we can make it," Cannon said.

"Did you ever have the feeling that something just wasn't going to work?" Eiler said. He looked at each of them, but more particularly at Fred Sheridan. "Have you talked to him?"

"I haven't gone near the stockade," Sheridan said. "What good would it do? I don't think you're going to break him, captain."

"So you've said before," Eiler murmured. "Nevertheless, we're going through with it. I want Whitlow to go first. Then you, Sheridan."

"Why me?"

"Because he once tried to kill you," Eiler said. "The idea is to jolt him and jolt him again. Mix him up. He's got to make a mistake."

"Because you want him to?" Sheridan asked. He lit a cigaret. "Captain, this whole thing is going bust on you. If Whitlow came your way what could he really say? That he saw Creel's hands while he sat behind those lamps?" Sheridan shook his head. "The judge knows that you have to present real evidence, not circumstantial."

"You're beginning to bother me," Cannon said pleasantly, and Sheridan quickly looked at him. Eiler's glance came up and he remained silent. "It ain't the things you do that bothers me," Cannon went on. "It's the things you don't do." He took out his tobacco sack and papers and talked while his fingers formed a cigaret. "Two years ago we had a fella in the stockade who solved his marriage problems with a hatchet. Seems he had three wives too many and just had to get rid of them. Newspaper fellas came from all over and one thing I noticed about them was that they just couldn't keep their nose out of anything." He paused to light his smoke. "Somehow, Sheridan, you don't have any curiosity at all."

"A man finds his stories in his own way,"

Sheridan said. "My editor is satisfied with my copy."

"What's your point?" Eiler asked.

"Charlie Dixon," Cannon said. "It's a funny thing about kids; people see 'em around but they don't pay any particular attention to 'em. Burke Pine must have known Dixon's kid, when he was five or six, but as a grown man, Pine wouldn't know him from Adam's off ox. But old Knapsack Gibbon, he knew Charlie Dixon the minute he saw him, and kept his mouth shut because his lifetime habits were too strong. Only Dixon didn't believe it would last. Anyway, he didn't want to take the chance, so he stuck a knife in the old man."

"We've already drawn that conclusion," Eiler said. "Why go over it, Jim?"

"Because no one's turned up with Charlie Dixon," Cannon said.

"Every sheriff in six states has been notified," Eiler said.

Cannon shook his head. "Let me put it together for you, and if you think I'm wrong, stop me. First, Knapsack came to the post before he went to town, so that means that Dixon saw him here, not in town."

"I don't see where you draw that conclusion," Rainsford said.

"Because," Cannon pointed out, "if Dixon saw the old man in town and recognized him, why did he kill him? Why didn't he just fade away? It was night and the street was dark where we found the old man. No, sir. Dixon knew he was on the hook because he was on the post when the old man was and the old man saw him. The recognition was mutual." He turned and looked at Fred Sheridan. "Figuring back, Charlie Dixon would be about your age now, wouldn't he?"

"You're going wild," Sheridan said. "Captain, you ought to give this man some leave. He's been working too hard."

"Don't push me off," Cannon said. "I don't push easy. Do you want me to stop, captain?"

"No," Eiler said. "Go on with it."

"He's got nothing to go on," Sheridan said and laughed.

"Yes I have," Cannon said, "and up to now it's bothered me considerable until I got it figured out. On the train to Kansas I read an article that you wired to your paper. You told all about Kyle Dixon's murder and how little Charlie escaped after the old man took him in tow. Where did you get that information, Sheridan?"

"Why, right here," Sheridan said. "You all know that."

"No, we don't know it," Cannon said. "Because when Knapsack told us that, you weren't in the room. You came in later, remember? But Charlie Dixon didn't need to be told because he already knew it."

"Smart," Sheridan said and vaulted out of his

chair. He bowled Colonel Lavery over and swung at Jim Cannon, who rolled out of the way, all the time trying to get his pistol from beneath the fold of his coat.

Sheridan bolted for the door and off the porch; he grabbed the first horse he found and pounded toward the gate while Eiler burst onto the porch, shouting, "STOP THAT MAN, GODDAMNIT!"

Sheridan was almost through the gate, well out of reach of anyone except the sentry by the guardhouse, and he flipped his Marlin to the shoulder and dropped Sheridan from the saddle even as Eiler screamed for him not to do that.

Then they were all running toward the downed man; Sheridan lay in the dust, shot through, thrashing his legs in spasms. Eiler could see that there was no hope; the guard's .40-82 had torn him open too horribly for surgical repair.

The sentry said, "I'm sure sorry, cap'n, but when you yelled to stop him—"

"It's all right, Bennett," Eiler said. "You did what any man would have done." He watched Sheridan's eyes film over, then said, "Get him carried over to the dispensary." He turned then and went back to his office, the others following him. On the way out he had snatched a pistol from his desk and he laid it on top and sat down and put his hands on his head. "He would have been our best witness. You broke him, Jim. It came as a surprise to me. It really did."

"The whole thing came to me while I was sittin' here," Cannon said.

"I read the article," Rainsford said. "I thought it very vivid and moving." He laughed briefly. "Damned sure simple to see why, isn't it?" He got up and went to the window and watched the evening come on. "Gentlemen, I confess that I'm tired and want to go home. I think you will agree that I've gone along pretty well with you on this whole affair, and I've given you ample time for you to prove your case for the State of Texas." He looked at Eiler. "Nathan, in the morning, I'm going to issue an order for the release of the prisoner."

Eiler's expression went slack. "Judge, you can't do that!"

Rainsford frowned. "Can't, Nathan? I'm going to pass over that because I know how keen your disappointment is. We just can't win them all, Nathan. Not even the important ones."

"But you know who the prisoner is!" Eiler shouted.

"Knowing who he is and convicting him are two different things," Rainsford said. "Now if you'll excuse me, I think I'll have supper and turn in early." He stepped to the door and paused there. "I—ah—wouldn't go through with this business in town tonight."

Eiler said, "Are you suggesting that Tass Creel would sue the State of Texas?"

199

"Stranger things have happened," Rainsford said and went out.

He ate in the mess tent, then stopped in to see George Whitlow, who was confined to the post, but not under close arrest. Whitlow was in his tent, playing solitaire and he nodded when Rainsford came in.

"I'd seen the Dixon kid many times," Whitlow said, "but I didn't recognize him as a man."

"Time distorts everything," Rainsford said. He lit a cigar, then offered one to Whitlow. "Dixon might just have been the man who could have broken Creel down. Too bad."

"It always is," Whitlow said. "But don't expect me to cry over it. I didn't want to go to the state pen." He laughed, and shuffled the cards. "But I wouldn't have been alone, would I, judge?"

"Likely not," Rainsford said. "No man, not even Price Shatlock, could have gotten so big without the blessing of men in power."

"You know it," Whitlow said. "Right to the governor's mansion. Some state senators have been nervous lately. A lot of others too."

"You might be interested to know that I'm issuing a release for McKitrick in the morning," Rainsford said.

"Best all around," Whitlow said. "Likely you have a friend or two who'd be pretty embarrassed to hear his name come up—"

Rainsford turned to the entrance. "That

wouldn't stop me, Whitlow. None of this will really stop me, or Nathan Eiler, or Jim Cannon. They've got Creel by the tail with a downhill pull and they'll never let go. Someday, sometime, every man makes his big mistake. They'll wait and they won't miss their chance when it comes. I only hope I'm on the bench when that time comes. You'll be there too, Whitlow. You see, you've only been given a short reprieve."

"Creel will be dead within three months," Whitlow said.

"Oh, that's probably true. Then we'll hang the man who kills him," Rainsford said and went out.

He could see the prisoner without a pass from Eiler, and the sergeant of the guard let him into McKitrick's cell. The man sat on his bunk, a lamp at his elbow, reading his borrowed Bible.

He looked up, then said, "It's a comfort to a man. A big comfort."

"You're being released in the morning," Rainsford said.

There was no expression of relief on the man's face. "My prayers have been answered. Yes, indeed they have."

"You've never prayed to anyone but the Devil, Creel."

"Why do you want to call me that?"

"Because that's your name," Rainsford said. "You know it and I know it."

"If that's so, why are you releasing me?"

"Because what we both know wouldn't stand up in a court of law," Rainsford said. "You're being set free, but we know who you are now. There'll never be any peace for you in this world, and damned sure none in hell, where you're bound."

"The Lord will protect me," McKitrick said and smiled benignly. Judge Rainsford clenched his fist and turned to the cell door; he stopped when Creel asked, "Did my money come yet?"

"Eiler would know. I wouldn't." He stepped outside and met McKitrick's sons on their way in; he didn't speak to them but walked rapidly, angrily to his own tent and laid down on the cot, too disturbed to sleep.

Later, he heard the sergeant of the guard challenge someone coming on the post, and then it was quiet again until an hour later when a ranger came to his tent and woke him.

"Sorry to bother you, judge, but Captain Eiler would like to see you in headquarters."

"All right," Rainsford said and ran his fingers through his hair. He walked across the parade and into the building. Eiler and Jim Cannon were there, and another man he had never seen before.

"I'd like to introduce Harry Fellows," Eiler said. "Judge Rainsford."

"A pleasure," Fellows said, smiling. He turned to Cannon as though completing a conversation interrupted by Rainsford's arrival. "Well, I got so interested, Jim, that I cut short my stay and took the train back." He swung his sharp glance to Rainsford. "Captain Eiler tells me you're releasing Creel in the morning."

"Yes, I am. Do you have any legal training, Mr. Fellows?"

"Enough to agree that you have nothing to stand up in court." He pulled gently at his lower lip. "A pity to have the bird almost in the pot and have him fly away." He shrugged. "You may get a second shot, but it will be much more difficult than the first. Creel will be on his guard constantly. Of course he'll kill again."

Rainsford stared. "No man would be that big of a fool."

"Well he can't help himself, you see," Harry Fellows pointed out. "He's mad. Completely mad. A man like that is swung like the phases of the moon."

"He asked me if his money had come yet," Rainsford said.

"I have it in the safe," Eiler said absently. Then he looked at Rainsford. "Did you go to the stockade?"

"Yes. I told him he was being released in the morning," Rainsford said. He saw the displeasure in Eiler's face, but there wouldn't be a discussion of it; he felt certain of that.

"That's a strange thing for a man to ask about,"

Harry Fellows said. "After all the emotional strain, he thinks of money."

"He drew out every cent he had in the Ashland bank," Eiler said matter-of-factly. "I sent the wire for him and—" He stopped and looked at Fellows. "Did you ever hear of a mad dog biting himself?"

"It's a novel thought, isn't it?" Fellows said. "The money obviously has a great significance to him." He pursed his lips and thought a moment. "Captain, he wouldn't know me at all, and I can play the Devil's advocate quite well."

"What do you think you're up to?" Rainsford asked.

"I want to see this man come completely unhinged," Fellows said. "If for no other reason than that it will be an excuse for continued confinement."

Rainsford shook his head. "I've had enough of this. Nathan, we're not making up our rules as we go along. If you can't come up with substantial evidence by morning, I'm issuing the release." He nodded to them and went out.

Fellows said, "A stubborn man."

"He's stretched his neck as far as it will go," Eiler said. "I can't blame him." A man's step crossed the porch and a ranger came in with a telegram.

Eiler casually glanced at it, then his jaw went slack as he read:

N. Eiler
Frontier Battalion
Rock Springs, Texas

Arriving 8:20 Friday with Tass Creel's wife and son. Cannon was right. Be an interesting meeting.

Pine

He passed it around for the others to read, then said, "By God, there'll be no release in the morning!"

"At least you can hold him for bigamy," Fellows said. "I seriously doubt he uses the name of Creel." He pulled at his lip again. "Captain, I think the dog is about ready to bite himself."

"By God, yes. I run this post," Eiler said. "Jim, have Creel brought here to the office." He sat and drummed his fingers on the desk, then Cannon came back, having told the guard on duty out front. "My uncle used to play the piano," Eiler was saying. "Everything by ear, you understand. Couldn't read a note. He'd hear a new tune, and once he'd heard a few bars he'd seem to know what was going to happen next and play right along. I think both of you know what we're after, and we'll play this just like Uncle Frank did the piano."

They waited, the ticking of the wall clock loud in the silence, then the prisoner was brought in.

Eiler said, "Sit down. That's all, Fleming. Close the door and resume your post."

"I guess you brought me here to apologize," the prisoner said. "I've been used hard, indeed I have." He looked at Cannon. "He hit me on the head with a rock when he took me prisoner. I've still got the scar." He jammed his hands in his coat pockets. "I want to thank you for the Bible, captain. It's been a comfort to me. I'll give it back before I leave in the morning."

"We've arranged a farewell party for you," Eiler said pleasantly. "We thought it was the least we could do for all the inconvenience you've been caused."

"Yes," Cannon said. "We'd like to invite your wife and boys. Both wives and your other boy."

The prisoner looked blankly from one to the other. "I don't know what you're talking about. I sure don't. I've only got one wife. And two boys."

"They'll be here tomorrow night," Eiler said. "Sergeant Pine has them on the train now. All the way from Piedras Negras, Creel."

"I'll bet it'll be a jolly party," Harry Fellows said. "The two women have never met, have they?"

They misjudged him completely for when he let go it took them by surprise. It began in his throat, in the bowels of the man, a whine of mortal torture, then he exploded from the chair, faster than they ever saw a man move, and Fellows was closest; he hit Fellows an axing blow and broke his jaw. Fellows was kited out of the chair and against the wall and Jim Cannon leaped on the man's back, but he was a bear, with a bear's angry strength; he hit backward with his elbow, caught Cannon alongside the head and sent him sprawling.

Eiler was digging for the pistol in his desk and the man whirled on him, and kicked him full in the forehead. The chair crashed back and Eiler lay groaning, conscious but unable to get up.

Cannon was trying to gain his feet and he went into him, shoulder into the ranger's stomach and he pinned him against the wall, driving the wind out of him. Then he had Cannon's revolver and crashed through the window to the ground outside.

The guard on duty outside rushed in as Cannon was getting to his feet. Eiler was groaning and trying to sit up, and his eyes were rapidly swelling shut.

"Get after him!" Cannon yelled and pawed in the desk drawer for the .45 Colt. He went through the window, sweeping aside broken glass with the gun barrel and the alarm triangle was being sounded and men ran out of their tents with lighted lanterns.

The first thing he established was that he was afoot; none of the horses were missing. The doctor came from the dispensary and went into headquarters while Cannon organized the search parties.

It all took time, fifteen minutes nearly, to get the company saddled and fanning out. He went inside headquarters. Fellows was still unconscious and Eiler was in a chair, his face covered with a thick, wet cloth.

"What a mess here," the doctor said.

"Cannon?" Eiler's voice was a pained mumble. "Jim, I want him alive."

"I told the men that," Cannon said. "He can't get far afoot."

"Find him," Eiler said. "Just find him."

"Yes, sir."

Cannon's horse was outside and he mounted up and started for town. His stomach was a solid ache and his breathing was painful, but he knew this would pass. Eiler's revolver did not fit Cannon's holster; the barrel was too long, and it was a .45 while Cannon's cartridges were .44s; he had five rounds for a dangerous man hunt and this didn't make him feel any better.

Creel would head for town, he felt sure, because it was the only place a man could hide. The prairie was no good. He'd need food and water and supplies and a horse and a town was the place to steal those things.

Mounted, Cannon knew he'd arrive ahead of Creel, and he needed that time to get the people off the streets and everything locked up; someone was sure to get killed and he wanted to keep the number down to the smallest possible figure.

The town was quiet when he got there and he found the night marshal and gave him the orders: clear the streets. Lock up all the places that are open. Cannon sat his horse and now and then rode up and down the main street while the lights went out. Two rangers rode in and sided Cannon. One of them crossed a leg over the saddle horn and rolled a cigaret.

"You sure broke up a good poker game," he said. "I was ahead a dollar and eighty-five cents." He started to scratch a match, then thought better of it and threw the cigaret away. "I never seen the town so dead."

"It'll liven up," Cannon said softly. "What caliber shells you got?"

"Thirty-eight forty," the ranger said. He looked across to the other man. "What you got, Shorty?"

"Forty-fours."

"It's not my night," Cannon said. He looked up and down the dark street. "Let's get the horses out of sight. Anyone else comin' in?"

Shorty shook his head. "They're out on the prairie. I guess he's all ours."

"He'll be all you can handle," Cannon said and led his horse into the alley and put him in a barn behind the feed store. Then he went back on the street to wait.

Chapter Thirteen

For better than an hour the town was grave-silent; no light showed anywhere and the only people on the street were the three rangers and they stayed along the walls of the buildings where the shadows were deepest. At the depot, the telegrapher sat at his key in a darkened room; he could not leave his post and at his left hand he kept his old army service revolver.

Beyond was a stretch of prairie bisected by the railroad tracks and miles out there appeared a bright glow that attracted their attention.

Finally Shorty dashed across the street to where Jim Cannon waited. "What do you make of that?" he asked.

Cannon studied the glow and watched it spread. "The prairie's afire. Still a little too green to have caught by itself." He wet his finger and held it up and found the night almost windless. "It could be one of the fellas is smokin' a rabbit out of his hole."

The fire grew brighter because it slowly grew nearer the town, but it did not build in intensity and from the new patches of brightness, Cannon guessed that the rangers were riding back and forth, relighting the prairie when the fires started to die down.

Cannon took out his watch and held it close to

his face and tried to make out the time: it was either ten minutes after twelve or two o'clock; he couldn't tell any closer than that. A few minutes later he looked again and found that a hand had moved to three, so he knew it was a quarter after twelve.

The prairie was bright with firelight for the patches of fire were no more than a mile from town, or perhaps a bit less; Cannon found it hard to tell exactly. A noise in the alley alerted them, and Shorty motioned to his partner and they both left their places.

One worked his way through a gap between the buildings while the other trotted around to the end of the street. Cannon crossed over so he could have a broad view of the other side and he waited.

Someone fired a shot and immediately there were two more, raggedly spaced, then someone stumbled and plunged clear of the space between the hardware store and the druggist's.

"Creel!" Cannon said. The man stopped near the hitchrack; Cannon could make him out clear enough for a shot, but he held back. "You'll never make it back to the buildings or across the street, Creel," Cannon said. "Do you want to die now?"

Creel waved his gun back and forth, trying to pick Cannon out, but he couldn't, and the other two rangers were moving in behind him.

He did what Cannon did not expect him to do;

he threw the gun into the dust and fell to his knees, hands thrust high above his head. "Don't shoot! God, don't shoot me!"

Two rangers rode into town and Cannon walked over to the man and picked up his own revolver. He holstered it, produced his handcuffs and snapped them on Creel's wrists. The man's clothes were torn and he was dirty with soot from the fire.

Shorty and his partner joined them in the street. Cannon said, "Get some lights on. Who did the shooting?"

"I did," Shorty said and seemed sorry that he had missed.

The rest was ranger business, getting the prisoner back to the post and the town put back to normal. The bulk of Eiler's company worked the rest of the night putting out the fire while Jim Cannon personally saw Tass Creel locked in his cell, and a double guard posted.

A light still burned in headquarters and Cannon went there. Captain Eiler was stretched out on the couch and his face was badly swollen; both eyes were completely closed and it would be a month before the effect of that one blow would leave him. He heard Cannon open the door, and Cannon said, "It's me, captain. The prisoner's been returned to his cell, sir."

"Good," Eiler said, his voice strained. "God, what a head I've got. This never should have happened, Jim, but I was so sure the three of us could handle him."

"Where's Harry Fellows?"

"The doctor's taking care of him," Eiler said. "A clean facture of the jaw." He reached out and groped for Cannon's arm. "There's going to be no damned release in the morning. You tell Rainsford that."

"Yes, sir," Cannon said and went out.

He was surprised to find Owen Henry and Judge Rainsford standing together by the porch; Henry said, "Thank God you didn't have to kill him, Cannon."

"What is he to you now, sheriff? Still your dear, harmless—"

"The judge has been telling me," Henry said impatiently. "I find it hard to believe. Very hard."

Cannon looked at Rainsford, then said, "The captain wants the prisoner held in the stockade."

"Yes, of course," Rainsford said softly. "I'll resume the hearing at ten o'clock in the morning. Good night, gentlemen." He walked away and Cannon remained a moment longer, then he walked toward the dispensary, and his route took him near the guardhouse.

The sentry on duty whistled and he went over.

"Cannon, you want to take a look at the prisoner?"

"Ain't I seen enough of him for one night?" Cannon said. Then he sighed. "All right."

The sentry unlocked the door and they went inside. A lamp burned in the outer office but the cell blocks were dark. From Creel's cell came the sounds of a man crying and the sentry spoke softly. "He's been doin' that for an hour. What do you make of it?"

"Conscience catching up with him," Cannon said and went out.

He was bone tired and his ribs ached from the scuffle in Eiler's office, yet he went on to the dispensary and found the doctor in his easy chair, eyes closed. When Cannon closed the door the doctor opened his eyes and reached for his pipe.

"I gave Fellows a sedative; he's feeling pretty good right now although the lower jaw has been immobilized." He arched an eyebrow. "The prisoner really went off his nut, didn't he?"

"In spades," Cannon said and went into the other room. It was a four-bed hospital that rarely lacked patients; Fellows was in the near bed and the lamp on his nightstand was turned down. He rolled his eyes to look at Cannon, then waved.

"What would you like to have me bring you?" Cannon asked. "Some taffy?"

"I loathe humor," Harry Fellows said. His voice was distorted because he could not move his jaw. "The doctor told me of Creel's recapture. Just gave up, huh?"

"Yep. Threw his gun down and quit."

"Strange," Fellows said. "The man's going to hang. Shooting would have been pleasanter."

"He must have run out of guts."

"Possible, but you know, none of this really fits. Damn it, my head's fuzzy."

"Try and get some sleep," Cannon said. "Rainsford's going to open the hearing in the morning. Maybe you'll feel well enough to look in."

"I'll be there if I have to be carried," Harry Fellows said.

The day dawned cloudy and by mid-morning a thin haze remained, making the day gray and hot and incredibly muggy. Rainsford called the hearing to order at ten o'clock and the prisoner, under heavy guard and wearing wrist and ankle chains, was taken to the mess tent, the only place on the post large enough to hold everyone.

Creel's wife and sons sat to one side and she wept continually and the boys sat with stony expressions. Owen Henry and Harry Fellows sat together, a bit to the rear of them, and George Whitlow sat behind them.

Rainsford rapped with a glass ashtray and brought the hearing to order and Cannon sat through it, through the lengthy legal phrasing of the state's purpose. Then there was the charge to the prisoner related to his rights, and the rules permitted in the presentation of the evidence.

He was glad to see the noon recess and didn't look forward to going back at two o'clock.

The afternoon was taken up by Nathan Eiler's testimony, the summation of information or evidence so far collected against the accused, but Cannon supposed this all had to be done. Eiler's reports were read to the court and at five o'clock, Rainsford adjourned until the next morning and Cannon got on his horse and went to town to spend the night with his family.

He felt a sense of foreboding, an emotional letdown and could not shake it. The wheels had somehow ground to a halt and he kept thinking that they really didn't have Creel, that somehow he would be dismissed. There was nothing to actually firm up this feeling, but it was there, a notion he couldn't shake.

It was as Harry Fellows had said, wrong, yet he could not pinpoint this subtle source of irritation.

When he returned to the post the next morning, the sergeant of the guard told him that Burke Pine was back and Cannon immediately went to Pine's tent and found the old man shaving. They shook hands warmly and Cannon sat down on the camp chair while Pine finished his shave.

"You had quite a vacation," Cannon said.

"A man that works as hard as I do deserves one," Pine said. He looked at Cannon and smiled. "How do you like the surprise I brought from Mexico?"

"Some surprise," Cannon said. "It broke Creel. Really broke him."

"Well, all that's left now is the identification," Pine said. "It's good to wrap up a case like this. We came close to not doin' it." He wiped his face and hung the towel. "Go ahead and ask me."

Cannon hesitated, then said, "Well, are you satisfied, Burke? He's going to hang for sure. Does it help?"

"Not a damned bit," Pine said and sat down. "I hear Creel's a broken man."

"There ain't much left of him to hang," Cannon said.

"Anyway, I want to look at him," Pine said and picked up his hat. "Comin' along?"

"Why not? We've rode the same way for some years. I'll go to the end with you," Cannon said.

Tass Creel sat in his cell and they stood there, looking through the bars at him and he didn't raise his head to see who was there. Lines had deepened in his face and he had lost some weight and the fight was gone.

Burke Pine said, "There ain't nothin' left," and walked out.

Cannon looked at his watch. "Time to get over to the mess tent, Burke." He looked at his friend. "Are you disappointed? You wanted him kicking and screaming, wanting to live and doomed to die. Creel don't care now."

"I just want to get it over and go fishing," Pine

said and walked on. They took seats somewhere around the left center and everyone stood up when Judge Rainsford came in. The hearing was brought to order and he looked at the prisoner. "Please rise and face the court." The two rangers flanking Creel poked him to get him to move and even helped him up.

Rainsford's eyes searched for Pine and found him. "Sergeant, will you escort the two witnesses into the tent please? They are in Captain Eiler's office."

Pine went out and a buzz of talk filled the tent. Sweat ran down Tass Creel's cheeks and he kept looking at Rainsford and the minutes passed this way, with everyone motionless and waiting.

Then Pine came back with the Spanish woman and her son. Rainsford said, "Madam, I am sorry to subject you to this distress, but I want you to identify the prisoner. Will you turn around, please?"

Everyone looked at her, including Creel, and Owen Henry started to get up, but Fellows took him by the arm and shook his head.

"HENRY!" she cried. "What are you doing here?"

She looked directly at Owen Henry and the prisoner gave a low moan and would have fallen had not the two rangers caught him. Instantly everyone started to talk, and Henry leaped from his seat, bowled over George Whitlow and would have made it clear out of the tent if Jim Cannon hadn't got in his way.

Cannon hit him in the fat softness of his stomach and Owen Henry's eyes got round and full of pain and he sat down with a thump and held his stomach, all the time struggling to draw in wind.

Pine, who was not far behind, took Henry's pistol and put it in his waistband. They hauled Owen Henry to his feet and forced him forward to the table where Rainsford sat. When Henry got close enough to the prisoner still being held by the two rangers he spat in his face.

Rainsford pounded for order and he got it. "I am done with this double identity, cloaked-in-mystery goings on. I am going to ask questions and I demand straight answers or it will go hard indeed!" He speared his finger. "You. What is your name? Not the name or names you go under, but your Christian name."

The two rangers had to poke again to get him to raise his head. "Moss Creel, sir. I changed it to McKitrick nearly twenty years ago."

He pointed to Owen Henry. "And you, sir?"

"Go to hell," Henry said.

Rainsford looked at Moss McKitrick. "Are you related to this man?"

"My brother," he said softly. "He's Tass Creel."

He tried to break away from Pine and Cannon to get to his brother, but they handcuffed him and forced him quiet. Rainsford said, "Sergeant, have this man placed under close guard. Corporal Cannon, clear the women out of this hearing place. The rest may remain." He glanced at the two rangers still holding onto Moss McKitrick. "Strike his irons and get a chair for him." He waited until this was done, then he looked at McKitrick. "There will be no evasion with me, sir. I'll ask the questions and you will answer. Is that clear?"

McKitrick nodded.

Rainsford said, "How long have you been aware of Tass Creel's activity?"

"Almost from the first," he said, looking at Rainsford. "But what could I do?"

"We may determine that," Rainsford said flatly. "You were seen in the vicinity of this town on the day Shatlock was killed. Will you explain that?"

"I knew what Tass was coming here to do and I wanted to stop him, but I was too late. I met him away from town, took the rifle and headed south hoping to draw the rangers off." He turned and looked at Jim Cannon and Burke Pine. "Up there in the rocks by the spring I missed you when I shot. My brother wouldn't have."

"Colonel Lavery identified your oldest son as looking like Tass Creel," Rainsford said. "Is there a resemblance?"

"He resembles Tass a great deal," Moss McKitrick said. "Even today, Tass and I favor one another. It worried me that you might notice it." He shook his head. "Judge, do we have to go into it now? For twenty years I've covered up, lived in fear this would happen. Could I rest awhile?"

Rainsford balanced in his mind the demands of the State of Texas against the lifetime sacrifice of this man. Then he rapped with the ashtray. "This hearing is adjourned. Mr. Creel—"

"Please, I want to be called McKitrick."

"Very well. You're free to join your wife. But don't leave town unless you have my permission." He rapped again and stood up and a few minutes later joined Cannon and Burke Pine outside. "Let's go to Eiler's office," he said and led the way.

Inside he lit a cigar and sat down and studied the tips of his shoes for a time. "It won't be hard now," he said. "All the answers will come now. Tass Creel will talk too. There's nothing he can hide."

"I know what was bothering me now," Cannon said. "The way Creel gave up in town. It didn't fit. Now it does. In the office, when he broke, it wasn't from guilt, but the weight of what he had carried for so long. For a time there he just lost his head."

"Yes," Rainsford said. "Why would a man do it? Go so far to cover for his brother? Do you suppose we'll ever know?"

"Moss McKitrick wasn't much of a success at

anything," Pine said. "He wasn't a good farmer. Maybe this was all he was good at." He looked glumly at Rainsford. "It must have been hell for him, knowing all these things and Tass Creel living there in the same town with him, parading the streets as a representative of the law and all the time being one of the most highly paid killers we've ever had."

"The wife that died in Kansas," Cannon said. "She was lucky. She never knew he had another in Mexico." He looked at Rainsford. "Judge, did you look at Moss McKitrick's face? What are we going to do about this man?"

"What can we do?" Rainsford said. "He's guilty as accessory and that's all there is to it."

He got up and stretched. "I'm tired and I'm going to catch up a horse and go for a ride and think this out. Tomorrow, when Tass Creel talks, men like George Whitlow are going to be running for cover. Have you ever seen a dam break? It'll be like that. A lot of warrants will be issued. You've done a good job."

"Haven't we though," Pine said.

"Burke, why don't you come home with me? Stay the night."

"Oh, I don't think your wife would want me underfoot," Pine said.

"Burke, I want you to do this for me," Cannon said.

Pine considered it, then said, "I guess I will. I

can't stand being alone either." He rubbed a hand across his face. "I don't want to look at the Spanish woman and know what this is costing her. I don't want to see McKitrick or his family again either."

"We are though," Cannon said. "You know that we've got to."

"I guess," Pine said and stepped to the door. He looked at the sky and the overcast that still lingered. "Looks like rain. Be good. Clears the air."

Then they stepped off the porch together and walked to the stable for their horses.

Center Point Publishing
600 Brooks Road ● PO Box 1
Thorndike ME 04986-0001 USA

(207) 568-3717

US & Canada:
1 800 929-9108
www.centerpointlargeprint.com